3pt.

2

Death of Lies: Socrates

by Margo Sorenson

Illustrations: Michael A. Aspengren

For Jim, Jane, and Jill, who always kept me going.
For Sue, good friend and editor-above-and-
beyond-the-call-of-duty.
For Suzanne who really knows how to ask those questions.

About the Author

Margo Sorenson was born in Washington, D.C. She spent the first seven years of her life in Europe, living where there were few children her age. She found books to be her best friends and read constantly. Ms. Sorenson wrote her own stories too. Her first one was called "Leo and Bo-Peep," which still makes her laugh today.

Ms. Sorenson finished her school years in California, graduating from the University of California at Los Angeles. She taught high school and middle school and raised a family of two daughters. Ms. Sorenson is now a full-time writer, writing primarily for young people junior high age or older. Ms. Sorenson enjoys writing for these age groups since she believes they are ready for new ideas and experiences, and they really enjoy "living" the lives of the characters in books.

After having lived in Hawaii and California, Ms. Sorenson now lives in Minnesota with her husband. She enjoys traveling to Europe and visiting places she might write about. When she isn't writing, she enjoys reading, sports, and traveling.

Text © 1998 by Perfection Learning® Corporation.

All rights reserved. No part of this book may be used or reproduced in any manner whatsoever without written permission from the publisher.

Printed in the United States of America.

For information, contact
Perfection Learning® Corporation,
1-800-831-4190,
1000 North Second Avenue, P.O. Box 500,
Logan, Iowa 51546-1099.
Paperback ISBN 0-7891-2156-5
Cover Craft® ISBN 07-807-6791-8

Contents

1

"I Ain't Wearing No Dress!"

"An F?" Aleesa gasped. She stared at the test paper on her desk.

But there it was. A big red F in Ms. Carter's block printing screamed at her from the top of the page.

"I couldn't have gotten an *F!*" Aleesa moaned. "Grandma will never let me out of the apartment again."

In front of Aleesa, Kenneth turned around. He snorted. "Yeah, right!" he said. "Like you actually studied all this Greek junk. You hated Socrates and all the philosophy stuff more than I did."

Kenneth shook his head and turned around. Aleesa always messed around in class. No wonder she got an F.

Kenneth tapped his pencil on his desk. What was *he* going to get on the test? He had to get a good grade. He sighed. His grades had to be passing to play football.

Aleesa made a face at his back. That Kenneth. He always thought he was right. So cool. Such a football stud. She crinkled up her nose.

Kenneth watched Ms. Carter stalk the aisles. She thrust test papers back at kids. All over the class, he heard groans and sighs. He glanced over at Natrone.

Natrone grinned. He held up his paper. He pointed to the grade at the top. "C+" it read.

Kenneth grinned at Natrone and gave him a thumbs-up sign. Relief washed over Kenneth. If Natrone got a C+, then he'd probably do much better. He sat up a little. Even though he hadn't studied either. This Socrates and Greek junk was pretty bad. He just didn't get it.

Who cared if the old chubby guy Socrates asked the Greek guys a lot of questions? The Greek guys didn't know the answers even. Those guys *all* looked stupid to him. Who cared about stuff like "What is truth? What is virtue?" anyway?

Kenneth tapped his pencil on his desk. Big deal. And back in those days, whatever it was B.C., everyone ran around in those dresses. Even guys. Those *were* dresses, Kenneth told himself. No matter what Ms. Carter called them. *Chitons* or something. Kenneth snorted to himself.

Aleesa slumped down in her desk. She crumpled up the test paper. Grandma was going to kill her. Aleesa squeezed the wad of paper hard. Could she throw it into the wastebasket from here? Her shooting was getting pretty good. Even her basketball coach said so.

Aleesa glanced over her shoulder. Uh-oh. Old Carter was right behind her. Probably giving Kenneth the A he always bragged about. Aleesa sighed. She dropped the wadded-up test on the desktop.

"And *this* was a surprise," Ms. Carter said. She laid the test paper on Kenneth's desk.

Kenneth turned it over. "F!" he blurted out. Stunned, he stared at the red printing at the top of the page. "There's gotta be a mistake," he said. What was he going to do about football?

Ms. Carter stopped passing out papers. She frowned over at Kenneth. "This wasn't like you, Kenneth," she said. "You usually study. But I don't think you understood the first thing about the Greek philosophers." She shook her head.

Aleesa tapped him on the shoulder. "So sorry about

the grade," she taunted. She pretended to wipe an imaginary tear from her eye.

Kenneth narrowed his eyes at her. "Fine for you to make jokes," he snapped. "Your grandma will just make you stay home from the mall. So you won't be able to pick up any guys for a while." A smile flitted across his face. Then he sobered. "But what am I gonna do about football?" He set his mouth. He turned back to look at Ms. Carter at the front of the class.

"A number of you didn't do well on this test," Ms. Carter was saying. "The quarter is almost over. For those of you worried about your grade, I have some options." She picked up a green marker. She began printing on the board.

"Extra Credit Choices," Aleesa read under her breath. She made a deep sigh. Maybe—maybe just this once, she'd better do extra credit. Grandma was already on her case. She grimaced.

Kenneth looked at the board. Extra credit, he groaned silently. He barely had time to get his regular homework done. Football practice. Baby-sitting his little brother Mason while Mom worked. But that F was going to hurt his grade. He puffed his cheeks out in frustration.

What looked easy? Aleesa wondered. She stared at the list on the board. Around her, kids were whispering. Lots of kids must have messed up on the test too.

There! Kenneth told himself. He printed out choice

#4 on his notebook. "Greek meal with conversation." Ms. Carter was blabbing on about what to do for each one.

"For number four," Ms. Carter was saying. "You go to the grocery store. You buy some Greek foods. Then you write a conversation. Pretend you are ancient Greeks in 399 B.C. You're having a dinner. From what you say, we should be able to learn something. Let us know about the ancient Greeks. Especially Socrates," she finished.

That's it, Kenneth told himself. He could get extra credit for just eating in front of the class. He could make up some conversation. It probably wasn't any big deal.

That looked easy, Aleesa thought. On her hand, she wrote in ink, "Greek meal with conversation."

"So who's interested in number four?" Ms. Carter asked. She looked at the class.

Kenneth's hand shot up. Behind him, Aleesa raised her hand at the same time.

"Wonderful," Ms. Carter said dryly. "Socrates would have loved it. Two opposites in a conversation. Kenneth and Aleesa—you may do number four." She printed "Kenneth and Aleesa" next to #4.

"What?" Aleesa blurted out. "Don't I get to choose who I'm with?" she asked. She couldn't work with Kenneth. What a jerk!

"Hey, Ms. Carter," Kenneth protested. "Can't I do this with someone else?" he asked. That Aleesa, he

9

fumed silently. One of the last people he'd ever want to work with.

Ms. Carter smiled. "It will be good for the two of you," she said. "Learn something about truth, honesty, and virtue from the Greeks. It will help the two of you get along. You should plan on going to the grocery store today after school. See what Greek food they have there. You can decide what to buy when it's time. But you need to get started today. It'll take you a while to write your conversation and plan your skit."

Kenneth heard Natrone snicker across the aisle. He gave Natrone a bad look. This was gonna be one of the worst days of his life. Natrone didn't have to make it worse. Going to the store with Aleesa. He almost groaned aloud. He put his head down on his desk.

From the corner of her eye, Aleesa saw Tyleene begin to jot down a note. It was probably to her. Tyleene would understand how she felt. Even though Tyleene thought Kenneth was cute.

But working with Kenneth! How could this have happened to her? Aleesa frowned down at her desktop. He just thought he was *it*. And going to the store after school? She kicked her foot against the desk leg. That was going to be really fun. Right.

Aleesa looked at the clock on the wall and sighed. School ended at three o'clock. Two hours till her death sentence.

At three o'clock, the bell rang. Kids stormed through the halls. Lockers clanged shut. Voices shouted.

"Yo! Trevor! Wait up!"

"Juleeeeea! Juleeeea! You didn't do it, did you?"

"Carletta, get *out!*"

Aleesa shoved two books into her locker. She zipped up her backpack.

"Ready?" a voice demanded behind her. Kenneth stood there, tapping his foot impatiently.

"Man!" Kenneth said, peering into the jumble of books and papers in Aleesa's locker. "Whatcha got in there?" He grinned wickedly. "An archaeological dig? Ruins from an ancient civilization?"

"Ha! Ha!" Aleesa snapped. She slammed her locker shut. She hitched up the straps of her backpack. "Let's get this over with, funny man. Hope you don't think you're gonna make a living telling jokes."

"You better be willing to work for this," Kenneth warned. He and Aleesa crossed the street against the light, dodging a car. "This is my grade you'll be messing with," he added darkly.

Kenneth and Aleesa walked into the grocery store. The automatic door whooshed behind them.

"Like I don't care about *my* grade?" Aleesa demanded. She made a face at him.

"Right!" Kenneth said. He laughed. "Ruin your straight A record, huh?" he jibed. He looked up at the

11

signs marking the store aisles. "Just remember," he added. "In that skit, I ain't wearin' no dress, though." He looked up. "International foods," he read aloud. "There."

"Okay," Aleesa pouted. "So my grades aren't as good as yours, hotshot," she mocked. "But I do have to keep them up. Or Grandma won't let me out of the house till I'm thirty."

"Well, just remember what I said," Kenneth said. "This is my football eligibility you're foolin' with."

They rounded the corner and stopped. A woman dressed in a flowing robe stood in the middle of the aisle. A garland of vines circled her hair. She stood behind a table holding plates of cheeses.

"Look!" Aleesa whispered. "Check it out! Weird outfit, huh?" she asked, grinning.

Kenneth glanced at Aleesa. He rolled his eyes. "That's one of those Greek outfits, dummy," he said. "Remember? The *chitons?* Even the guys wore them." He snickered. "I wouldn't wear any dress. Tell you that!"

"Taste some imported Greek cheeses?" the woman called to them. She held out a plate stacked with squares of a white cheese.

"Yeah, sure. Why not?" Kenneth asked. "I'm kinda hungry." He walked over and took a piece of cheese. He popped it into his mouth. It had a funny tang to it. He poked at it inside his mouth with his tongue. It tasted strange.

"Okay. Me too," Aleesa chimed in. She took a piece and put it into her mouth. Whoa! she thought. That was a different taste! She stared at the woman.

Why did the woman have such a funny smile on her face? Oh, my gosh! Aleesa thought. She blinked. Everything started to blur. The store began to reel. She grabbed Kenneth's arm.

"What's happening?" she croaked.

"I don't know!" Kenneth choked out. His ears rang. The woman looked at him and smiled knowingly. What was going on? The store got dark. Then it got light. Blindingly bright.

Still holding Kenneth's arm, Aleesa gasped. Bright light stunned her. She looked around. The store was gone! Where were they?

Kenneth blinked. The store had disappeared. What had happened? He looked around, wildly. Then he glanced down at his clothes. His shirt and Levis were gone. And in their place—

"Hey!" he yelled. "I ain't wearin' no dress!"

2

Socrates the Menace

Aleesa stared at Kenneth. Her jaw dropped. He *was* wearing one of those Greek dress things! What had happened?

"You're wearing one too!" Kenneth exclaimed. Would people laugh at him dressed like this? He brushed angrily at the folds of the robe.

Aleesa looked down and gasped. What was going on?

Then Kenneth looked around them. His hair lifted at the roots. Where were they?

Aleesa followed Kenneth's gaze, staring open-mouthed. The grocery store was gone. They were in some kind of an open market. It looked like the farmers' market back home. But really different. Really, really different. Goose bumps ran up and down her arms. Something was wrong! This wasn't anywhere close to Berkeley, California!

Dozens of people dressed in *chitons* sat beside displays of vegetables, fruits, and cheeses. Other people strolled up and down the rows, looking and buying. They were wearing those Greek *chitons* too. They all looked like the pictures of the old Greeks in her textbook.

There were no cars. There were no streetlights. No neon signs. And the buildings looked really old! Like the movies they watched on ancient Greece. Aleesa shivered.

"Kenneth," Aleesa managed to say. "Tell me we're not where I think we are!" she begged. Her face twisted with worry.

Kenneth blinked. He rubbed his eyes. Nothing changed. He looked at Aleesa. His heart pounded. "I . . . I'm afraid we are . . .," he croaked hoarsely. "In ancient Athens."

"Now what do we do?" Aleesa's voice rose to a wail. "I want to go back home! I don't care if Grandma grounds me for life!"

"Shhhhh!" Kenneth warned. He glanced around them.

A passing man stared at them for a second. But then he went on his way.

"We can't let anyone know who we are," Kenneth said in a low voice. "Who knows what these Athenian guys might do to us." He leaned closer to Aleesa. "Remember what they did to Socrates?"

Aleesa's eyes widened. "Oh, my gosh! They killed him!" she said. She wrung her hands. "I don't want to die! I'm too young!" she moaned.

"They gave him a trial first, dummy," Kenneth said. Then he frowned. "But he still was sentenced to death. We'd better be really careful." He looked around again. "We've got to figure out how to get back home."

"Before anyone finds out we don't belong here," Aleesa agreed. "But how?" she asked.

"There you two are!" a hearty voice said behind them.

Startled, Aleesa and Kenneth jumped. They whipped around. An older man, dressed in a *chiton,* stood smiling. He was holding two large baskets. He held them out to Aleesa and Kenneth.

Aleesa glanced quickly at Kenneth. Kenneth swallowed hard. He reached out. He grabbed a basket. Aleesa followed his lead. She took the other basket.

"Better not let my son Tisander see you not working," the man said wryly. "You know how he felt about my hiring you two. He told me to just use slaves." The man shook his head. "He said, 'Don't pay *metics,* Father. They'll just want to go home again.' "

"Yeah!" Aleesa blurted. "Home!" Yes! They wanted to go home! "Yeah! We want—"

Kenneth broke in. *"Metics?"* he asked. He gave Aleesa a little kick with his sandal. He glared at her. She'd better not mess up. She couldn't ask to go home. People would start asking questions. They'd get in trouble. Who knew what would happen?

Aleesa made a face back at Kenneth. How could he kick her like that? What a jerk!

"Yes, *metics,*" the man repeated. He looked at them strangely for a moment. Then he smiled. "Oh! Of course. You wouldn't know that word. *Metic* means an *alien.* Someone who isn't Athenian. Someone from another city-state or country. You're from Ionia, right?" he asked.

"Right," Kenneth said quickly. He jabbed Aleesa with his elbow. She made another face at him.

"Anyway," the man went on. "We have to finish the shopping here at the *agora.* Then you can go back to my pottery shop. Eurmikos can show you how to make the handles for the *hydria.*"

"Great!" Kenneth said. *Hydria?* What were those? They sounded like some kind of poisonous snake. But they must be pots or something. He said pottery shop, didn't he?

17

"Great," Aleesa said. She shrugged her shoulders at Kenneth. Okay. So she'd just follow along. For now, anyway. But Kenneth had better not get them into any trouble. He always told her *she* was the one who caused trouble. He had better watch his step too. He sure wasn't perfect.

Kenneth and Aleesa followed the man. He stopped at a fruit display.

Aleesa looked at the fruit. There was a lot of stuff she hadn't even seen before. Her mouth felt dry. How were they going to keep from being found out?

"Greetings, Laios," the woman said. "Some oranges today?"

Laios, Kenneth thought. That was this guy's name. At least they knew that much.

He tugged at Aleesa's robe. He jerked his head to the right. They stepped away from Laios. Laios was bargaining with the woman.

"Okay," Kenneth whispered. "So we're aliens—"

Aleesa giggled. She felt the top of her head. "I don't have green horns!" she teased. "I didn't come in any spaceship!" Or did they? she wondered for a second. She shivered.

Kenneth frowned. "Knock it off," he snapped. He glanced over at Laios again. But Laios was still busy talking. "Let's figure out what we know. We work for this guy Laios in a pottery shop he owns. Laios has a son,

Tisander. Tisander didn't want his father to hire us. So we'd better watch out for him."

"Yeah," Aleesa breathed. "That Tisander guy wanted slaves instead," she said. "Didn't Laios say something about slaves?" She shuddered.

"Remember?" Kenneth asked. He shook his head in disgust. "You really deserved that F on the test," he said. "They had slaves in ancient Greece. When the Greeks fought and won, they'd make slaves of the people they beat in the war."

"Will they make *us* slaves?" Aleesa asked. A twinge of fear rippled through her.

"Naaah," Kenneth said. He hoped he sounded more sure than he felt. "We may not be citizens of Athens. But we're not slaves. We're *metics,* remember?"

"How are we going to get back home?" Aleesa asked. She looked over at Laios.

"I don't know yet," Kenneth muttered. "We'll figure it out." He swallowed hard. They had to get home. Before they got caught. And something really bad happened.

Laios dropped some oranges in Aleesa's basket. "Let's go on," he said. Aleesa and Kenneth followed Laios. They threaded their way through the crowded marketplace. Voices called out. Talking and laughing filled the air. Strange, exotic smells drifted by them.

"Laios!" a voice cried out. A burly man grasped Laios's arm. Laios smiled.

"*Hail,* Bion," Laios said. Aleesa and Kenneth stopped.

Bion looked around him carefully. Then he came close to Laios. "What do you hear about the charges against Socrates?" he asked in a low voice.

The charges? Socrates? A chill of fear ran through Aleesa. Did that mean they were in Athens at the time of Socrates? And Socrates wasn't dead yet? She whipped around to look at Kenneth. He was holding a finger to his lips, frowning at her.

"Shhhh!" Kenneth whispered. Aleesa had better not say anything. Socrates hadn't died! Could . . . could they do something about this? Could they stop him from being killed?

Laios was shaking his head. "I am worried, friend," he said. "Socrates has made many enemies. He makes people feel uncomfortable. But that's not a crime. Anytus, Meletus, and the other leaders know that. They'll have to make up a charge that the council—the citizens in the *boule*—will think is a crime. Then the *boule* will vote him guilty."

Bion nodded. "Yes. You speak the truth," he said. "It looks bad for Socrates that two of his close friends, Alcibiades and Critias, turned out to be evil men. Traitors to Athens. Makers of a bloodbath. But Meletus can't say that in the charges against Socrates. Meletus can't say Socrates taught them to be evil. He can't say that because of the amnesty."

"What's that?" Aleesa whispered to Kenneth. She poked him. "Amnesty?"

"Uh—like a pardon for a crime," Kenneth answered quickly. "Shhhh! Listen," he urged. "Maybe they'll talk about it."

Aleesa made a face. But she tilted her head and listened some more.

Laios sighed. "You are right. No one can be charged for those crimes. That was four years ago. So they can't even talk about Alcibiades and Critias, those traitors. Besides, who would have guessed it? Alcibiades turning into a traitor? When he went to Sparta, he told them our secrets." He frowned. "That helped Sparta defeat us."

"And how about Critias too?" Bion asked.

"Later," Laios said quickly. He looked to the right. He frowned. "Here comes my son, Tisander." He shook his head. "Tisander and his friends don't need any more encouragement to hate Socrates." He set his mouth for a moment. "I cannot talk any sense into that young whelp."

Aleesa stared at Kenneth. There was a lot of stuff happening here. She yanked at his robe.

"Come here," Aleesa hissed. "What's all that about?"

"How do I know?" Kenneth asked. He moved closer. "I got an F on the test too, remember?" he jibed. Then his face got serious. "But it sounds like some guy is going to make up lies about Socrates. So the council will judge him guilty."

Aleesa glanced at the two men. Laios and his friend Bion waited for a young man swaggering toward them. Four young men walked with him.

Uh-oh, Kenneth thought. It looked like trouble. If the main guy was Tisander, it looked like he had a bad attitude.

"What was that junk about traitors?" Aleesa whispered. "And even Laios's son doesn't like Socrates? Wasn't Socrates supposed to be a good guy? I thought I remembered *that* much from class," she said in a low voice.

"I don't know either," Kenneth answered back softly. "Let's hear what's going on."

Kenneth and Aleesa moved a little closer to Laios and Bion. Tisander and his small group of friends exchanged greetings with the men.

"So!" Tisander challenged. He jutted his chin in the air. "Socrates will be charged this afternoon. And it's about time." He stared insolently at his father.

Laios frowned. "Do not speak about things you know nothing of," he demanded. "You are not a member of the *boule*. You do not have a vote. You are yet a youth."

"Ha!" Tisander laughed. He elbowed one of the young men next to him. His friends rudely echoed Tisander's laughter.

"That doesn't matter," Tisander said. "Socrates is a traitor. Everyone knows it." He glanced around at his friends. They listened eagerly, Aleesa noticed.

"Socrates deserves to die," Tisander sneered. Then he stared right at Aleesa and Kenneth.

"Don't you think so too?" Tisander challenged them.

3

Socrates!

Aleesa and Kenneth stared at each other. Now what? Kenneth asked himself. What could they say?

"I'm warning you—" Laios thundered. He stopped short. He tightened his mouth. Then he shook his head and sighed. "These two are not citizens. Keep them out of this."

Tisander kept staring at Kenneth and Aleesa. He narrowed his eyes. He looked them up and down.

Kenneth thought how he'd like to punch this guy. He doubled up his fists behind his back.

What a jerk! Aleesa snapped silently. She'd like to slap Tisander.

"The *metics*," Tisander sneered. "I hope you're not spending too much money on them," he complained, turning to Laios. "You could get slaves to do the same work. For nothing."

Laios wheeled on him. "You watch your insolent mouth," he barked. "I will handle the affairs of the household."

Laios turned to Aleesa and Kenneth. "I apologize for my son," he said. "He forgets who he is these days."

Laios glared at Tisander. "I will settle with you later. Take your—friends—and go. I have work to do."

Aleesa and Kenneth watched Tisander and his friends saunter away. Tisander tossed his head. They could still hear his rude laughter.

He'd make sure Tisander and his friends stayed away, Kenneth promised himself. He'd just as soon take the guy out, like in football.

Aleesa scrunched up her face. What a slimeball! She could think of a lot of things she'd like to tell Tisander. And they wouldn't be things Grandma would be happy to hear her say either.

Laios shook his head. "Tisander has fallen under bad

influence," he muttered. Then he looked at Kenneth and Aleesa. "He should talk with Socrates again. Socrates would ask him more questions. He'd make Tisander really think about what he's doing." Laios laughed shortly. "Tisander wouldn't like it. He didn't like it when Socrates talked to him before either. But maybe he'd find out the right way to act."

"Yes, friend," Bion said. "Tisander wouldn't like it. No one *likes* to answer difficult questions. No one likes to look inside himself."

"Socrates makes you see the truth," Laios explained to Aleesa and Kenneth. He cleared his throat. "Not many people enjoy that."

No kidding, Aleesa thought. She shivered. The Athenians killed Socrates because of it.

Kenneth looked at Laios. He swallowed hard. That was the truth, all right. People sure didn't like to answer hard questions. That's why they put Socrates to death. But Laios didn't know that yet. No one knew that—except him and Aleesa. His stomach tightened.

"Well, I'll send you on to the *cerameikos*," Laios said. "The pottery quarter. My shop is in that section of town."

What? Aleesa almost squeaked aloud. They had to walk around ancient Athens? By themselves?

Kenneth stiffened. Great. He'd have to pay attention. They'd better not get lost in Athens. Or they'd really have a problem.

What if somebody kidnapped them? Then they'd have to become slaves. He'd seen that in a movie once. Guys getting dragged away and put in chains. He held back a shudder.

Laios pointed to a building with stone pillars in the front. Around the pillars, small bunches of men stood talking. What were they talking about? Aleesa wondered.

"Hey," Aleesa said. She nodded toward the building. "How come all those men are standing around talking? Everyone sure talks a lot around here." She gestured to other men grouped around the marketplace. Everyone seemed to be in conversation.

"Ah," Laios said. He smiled. "In Ionia, you probably don't do as much socializing as we do," he said. "In Athens, it's important to talk to others. Because we have a democracy, we need to talk about our ideas for the government. We need to talk about the laws."

Laios pointed to the blue sky above them. "Besides, our weather is always nice. So we can be outside often. We discuss great ideas too. Like what is truth? What is justice? How do you live a good life?" He smiled. "The things Socrates asks us to think about."

Huh, Aleesa snorted silently. Going to the mall sounded like a lot more fun. It all sounded pretty strange to her. But no wonder everyone knew about Socrates. Guys just stood around talking all the time. Weird.

"Turn right at that *stoa*," Laios said. He gestured toward the building again. "Then walk until you see my shop. Remember, a big black jar stands next to the doorway." He took their baskets. "I'll send someone else home with the rest of the food I'll buy." He raised a hand. "Farewell," he said.

"Farewell," Aleesa and Kenneth said together. They turned and began walking.

Aleesa took a deep breath. "I hope this is going to turn out okay," she said. "I don't like this at all. Not one bit. I just want to get back home!" She looked around the *agora*. "Do you see anyone selling cheese? Like that woman in the store?" she asked. Her face scrunched with worry. "Do you think that's how we can get back home? *If* we can get back home?"

"I want to go home too," Kenneth said. "But listen! Think about it." He grabbed Aleesa's sleeve. "Think about what Laios said. Socrates is being charged today. With his so-called crimes. Whatever they are. He isn't dead yet. Maybe we could try to save Socrates!" He looked at Aleesa intently.

"But we can't change history, can we?" Aleesa asked. She shook Kenneth's hand off her sleeve. "We can't do anything about it."

"We don't know that," Kenneth said darkly. "Remember reading in science class?" he asked. "Remember about the black hole. Scientists think some black holes fall inside themselves. And that time has no meaning in them." Kenneth lowered his voice. He stared at Aleesa. "You can travel backward and forward in time. That means you could meet your own parents when they were kids! You could even change stuff that happened!"

"No, thank you!" Aleesa said. She swallowed hard. "I like being right where I am in Berkeley. Even with Grandma."

"But think about it, Aleesa," Kenneth said. They stopped at the *stoa*. "We got here, didn't we?" He gestured around them. "In ancient Athens. And do you know how to speak Greek?" Aleesa shook her head mutely. "So how are we able to talk to everyone?" Kenneth asked. "Huh? What do you think all this could mean?" The hair rose on his arms at the sound of his own words. This *was* really weird.

"I don't know," Aleesa wailed. "All I know is I want to go back home. I don't know why we should try to save Socrates. We might get killed too. And what about someone deciding to make slaves of *us?* " she blurted out.

"Shhhh!" Kenneth said quickly. He looked around them. The men still talked in quiet groups in the *stoa*. No one had heard. "Let's get going. Let's see if we can find out anything else," he said. "We need to find out where Socrates is. Maybe we can warn him."

Kenneth began walking. Aleesa caught up with him.

"People in the pottery shop might talk about Socrates," Kenneth said. "Everyone's talking about him today. They're wondering what the charges against him will be."

"Okay," Aleesa grumbled. "But there'd better be a really good reason to try to save him. I'm not gonna just risk my life for nothing. I mean, I know he's supposed to be a good guy." She made a face. "But I sure don't know why. I mean, who cares? A bunch of guys standing around, answering questions. Puh-lease. It was sure boring in class."

"Your test grade proved that!" Kenneth joked. He began walking faster.

"I didn't see *you* getting any A, Einstein," Aleesa taunted. She flipped her bangs out of her eyes.

"Yeah, yeah," Kenneth muttered. "I know what you mean about going home though," he agreed. "Would you look at these?" he asked. He pointed to his feet. "Look at these things. These weird sandals on my feet!"

Kenneth kicked a loose pebble in the street. He whacked the skirt of his *chiton.* "And *this!* " he exclaimed in disgust. "This is the worst!"

Aleesa giggled. "Yeah," she teased. "You'd look great going out for a pass in *that* outfit!"

"Hey!" Kenneth said. He tried to grab Aleesa's arm. But she giggled and dodged him.

Kenneth and Aleesa turned a corner. They walked into the *cerameikos* section.

"Look at all this stuff!" Aleesa said. She stopped in the middle of the narrow street. All around them, through open doorways, she could see people working. Inside shops, people shaped clay. Potters threw pots on wheels. Some people painted vases. Some lined pots up on racks to bake in kilns.

"And that must be Laios's shop," Kenneth said. Ahead, a huge vase stood next to a doorway. The vase was black.

"What's the decoration painted on it?" Aleesa asked. She walked closer. "Look," she said. She touched the side of the vase. "Look at all the people painted in red. They're dancing and stuff." She grinned. "It looks just like the pictures in our textbook! From the museum."

"Shhhhh!" Kenneth said. He frowned. "You don't know who's listening. You can't let anyone hear you say stuff like that. They don't even have books yet. Or museums." He shook his head. "I guess we'd better get inside. I hope we don't have to paint people that look like that," he said. "Guys wearing dresses." He sighed.

"Now you be quiet," Aleesa warned. "See? You could get us in trouble too." She scrunched her face up at Kenneth.

"You don't even know what you're talking about," Kenneth snapped. He set his jaw. He took a deep breath. They had to do this. They had to walk into the shop and do a job. He walked through the open doorway.

Aleesa swallowed hard. She followed Kenneth into the shop.

Many people were working inside. Craftsmen painted. Some shaped pots. Some used a tool on vases.

Loud talking filled the air. A fine ceramic dust sifted over everything.

"Ah—Eurmikos?" Kenneth called out over the noise. "Is Eurmikos here?"

An old man with a beard walked up. He looked at Kenneth and Aleesa. He smiled.

"I am Eurmikos," the old man said. "You must be the *metics* Laios hired," he said. "Good. You can help put handles on the *hydria.*" He pointed to a vase that was still unbaked clay. It had no handles. "Like this." Then he pointed to another vase. This vase was painted black. It had three handles. Weird, Kenneth thought.

An hour later, Kenneth and Aleesa sat at a low table. They coiled damp clay onto vases.

"Whew!" Aleesa said. She wiped her forehead. "My neck hurts. My arms are sore. And I'm getting tired."

"All you do is complain," Kenneth snapped. He rotated his shoulders one at a time. He leaned back his head. "Good thing you don't play football. You'd never make it. It's a miracle you lasted on the basketball team," he added in a low voice.

Just then, voices called out in the shop.

"Socrates!" someone said loudly.

"*Hail,* Socrates," another voice called.

"Socrates?" Aleesa gasped. A shiver ran down her spine. This was unreal. Were they really going to see Socrates?

4

Socrates the Bad Guy?

A short, chubby man with a round stomach stood in the doorway. He had a pug nose. He had pop eyes. Workers crowded around him. He was smiling at everyone.

"Well, he's no prize," Aleesa snorted. "He's kind of ugly, isn't he? Are you sure that's Socrates?"

"Yeah," Kenneth said. He held the moist clay tightly. He couldn't believe it. Here he was, looking at one of the most famous guys in history.

"Well, Socrates," one of the men said. "You're supposed to be a great thinker, right?"

"No," Socrates said with a smile. He shook his head. "In fact, I am the most ignorant of men. I know that I have much to learn."

That's pretty rare, Kenneth thought, staring at Socrates. Not many people would admit that.

"But Socrates," the man persisted. "You can prove things to be true when you want to, right?"

"Perhaps," Socrates answered. He smiled gently. "Although you know I prefer to ask questions about truth, virtue, and goodness. We must find out what the true good is for man. When we know what the good truly is, we can *be* good. But," he chuckled, "I will play your little game today."

"Well, then, prove that you are more handsome than I," the man said with a laugh. "Use your famous logic."

"Good luck," Aleesa whispered to Kenneth. "No way is Socrates better-looking than that guy."

"Well," Socrates began. A hush fell over the room. The potters stopped the wheels.

"Oh, my gosh," Aleesa whispered. "Are we really gonna hear one of those dialogue thingies we read about?"

"It sounds like it," Kenneth said. He was going to actually hear the great Socrates in action! He felt goose bumps on his arms. This was wild.

"Does beauty exist in only one thing?" Socrates asked.

"No. In many things," the man answered. "Shields. Spears. Swords."

"But how can all of those be beautiful?" Socrates continued. "They don't look like each other, do they?"

"No," the man replied. "But they are made well for their purposes. That's why I can call them beautiful. If something does its job well, it's beautiful."

"Ah," Socrates said. People in the group began to smile. "Then what are eyes made for?" he asked.

"Well, to see with," the man said. He shrugged his shoulders.

"In that case, my eyes are more beautiful than yours," said Socrates. "They are better made for the purpose of seeing. Your eyes look only straight ahead. But my eyes bulge out. So I can see better to the side too!" He grinned.

Everyone in the shop laughed. Even the man who'd lost the argument. People slapped each other on the back.

"That was amazing," Kenneth said. He blinked. Then he looked at Aleesa. "How he could prove something like that? Just by asking questions?" He shook his head in wonder.

"Yeah," Aleesa agreed. "Wish I could do something like that with Grandma! That would change *my* life!" She giggled. "Think what I could do!" Then her grin faded.

"If we ever get home, that is." She squished the coil of clay against the vase and sighed.

Laughing, Socrates left the shop. People fell back to work. The sound of the potters' wheels sliced through the air again. The hum of conversation went on.

"Has my father been here?" a voice asked loudly. Kenneth turned around. He frowned. That's what he was afraid of. Tisander and his friends lounged against the shop door.

"No," Eurmikos called. Kenneth watched Eurmikos. He set his mouth and kept walking around the shop. He stood behind each worker for a while. He'd murmur a comment and then move on.

"I thought I saw that traitor Socrates in here," Tisander challenged. His friends snickered.

"Perhaps. We're all busy," Eurmikos answered. He leaned over. He scraped some loose clay off a vase.

"You know he deserves to die," Tisander said loudly. His friends nodded their heads.

What a bunch of losers, Kenneth thought. He looked over at Aleesa. She looked as if she was ready to throw a lump of clay at them.

"Don't any of you remember Critias? Socrates' *good* friend?" Tisander asked. "Critias turned Athens into a bloodbath. Just four years ago, when he was the leader of the revolution."

Tisander stopped and looked around. The workers kept their heads down. No one watched him.

Tisander frowned. "None of you remember men murdered in the streets?" he asked. "All because of Critias? And who was his teacher? None other than Socrates."

Tisander spit onto the dirt floor of the shop. Aleesa jumped. She frowned down at the clay. Kenneth set his mouth. Tisander really hated Socrates.

"Socrates is a traitor. He is friends with traitors. Alcibiades and Critias brought death to Athens. We should bring death to Socrates!" Tisander exclaimed. He slammed his fist into his open palm. "Maybe he can talk his way out of the charges. If so—" He stopped. He glanced at his friends. "If so, maybe we'll have to take matters into our own hands."

The pottery shop was silent. Just the humming of the wheels cut through the still air. No one would meet Tisander's angry eyes. The workers glanced at each other. Kenneth saw some of them roll their eyes.

"Whoa!" Aleesa breathed. "Tisander is pretty mad!" She formed a clay coil with her fingers.

"No kidding," Kenneth muttered under his breath. "He's crazy too." He thumped some clay on the table.

"No one has anything to say to me?" Tisander snorted. "Well, fools will stay together. You're all just as foolish as my father. Come," he said to his friends. "It's time to go to the gymnasium and throw the discus." He tossed his head. He marched out the door. His friends trailed after him, snickering.

"Socrates didn't really teach those guys to kill, did he?" Aleesa asked. She looked at Kenneth. "To become traitors? You know. Alci-whoever and Critias?"

"Are you kidding?" Kenneth spluttered. "You heard Socrates yourself, right? You've heard Laios and his friend talk about Socrates too. Socrates is a good man. He would never stand behind murder. He's for truth and goodness and virtue. Those guys just probably went bad all on their own. Some people hate Socrates for another reason, it sounds like to me."

Kenneth frowned as he coiled some clay around a handle. He smoothed the coil down. He looked back at Aleesa.

"No one talks about the real reason they hate Socrates. It's because they don't like to find out they're idiots, that's all," Kenneth continued. He slapped some more clay on the table, hard.

"Well, what crimes will Socrates be charged with?" Aleesa asked. "That he makes people embarrassed? Because they don't know as much as they think they do? That can't be."

Aleesa curled a strip of clay around the *hydria's* handle. She shaped it with her fingers. She looked over at Kenneth, waiting for his answer. But he was frowning at the *hydria* in front of him. He began scraping at one of the handles with the tool.

"Okay. Fine. I'll ask Eurmikos then," Aleesa snapped. "He'll know the answer. I'm tired of asking questions and hearing you say you don't know," she complained. She stood up. "Eurmikos!" she called. "I have a question."

Kenneth tugged at Aleesa's robe. "Sit down, you cabbage brain," he snapped. "Eurmikos might find out we don't really belong here in Athens. And then what?" He shook his head in exasperation. He saw Eurmikos walking toward them. "You've really done it this time," he muttered.

Kenneth lay down the clay coil on the tabletop. He looked around. What if they were found out now? All because of Aleesa and her big mouth. How could they escape if they had to? Could they run out the door of the shop?

"Yes?" Eurmikos asked. He stood in front of them. He looked at Aleesa's *hydria*. Then he looked at Kenneth's. "Not bad," he said. He traced the handles with his finger. "Not bad for beginners." He smiled. "You had a question?" he asked.

"Yeah," Aleesa said. She took a deep breath. "Okay. You know Socrates?" she began.

"The finest man in all of Athens. In all of Greece," Eurmikos said. "What is it?"

"Well, you know that guy Tisander?" Aleesa searched Eurmikos's face. He nodded as Aleesa continued. "Tisander said Socrates was a traitor. For teaching some guys to murder or something. And then I heard something about amnesty. So—" Aleesa stopped and sighed. "Can you explain this to me? What crimes can they charge Socrates with?" she asked. "Sorry I don't know anything. I'm just a *metic*," she added.

Aleesa shot a smug glance at Kenneth. See? She could handle things.

Eurmikos smiled. "First, Tisander is wrong," he said. "Socrates cannot be blamed for what his friends did. He never taught them to kill. Or to turn traitor. True, some people are afraid of Socrates. But they're not afraid of him for *that* reason. And fear is a strong feeling. It makes people do rash things."

Eurmikos sighed. He stroked his beard.

"But even so, Socrates cannot be blamed for the horrible things Critias and Alcibiades did," Eurmikos said. "Critias and Alcibiades were given amnesty. They have been pardoned. So even if Socrates did have anything to do with their crimes, it wouldn't matter. No one can be charged *now* with any crime that happened back *then*. Everyone's been pardoned. But people still try to use that as an excuse to get rid of Socrates."

"Well, I still don't get it," Aleesa complained. "So what will the council say Socrates did wrong? And why are people after him? Why do they want to punish Socrates?" She folded her arms. She looked at Eurmikos.

Kenneth drew a breath. He winced. Why couldn't Aleesa just be quiet? Why did she have to keep going on and on about this?

"Surely you must have heard that Socrates has made many enemies," Eurmikos said. "Even *metics* would have heard that," he said. He looked at Aleesa and Kenneth curiously.

Uh-oh, Kenneth thought. Was this going to be trouble? He kicked Aleesa under the table.

"Ouch! Uh, yeah, sure," Aleesa said quickly. She darted a furious glance at Kenneth. She leaned down and rubbed her ankle.

"Socrates' only crime is that he makes people too uncomfortable. They don't like to face the truth," Eurmikos said. "And there's a good reason why."

Kenneth saw Eurmikos look around the pottery shop. Everyone was busy. No one was listening. Eurmikos pursed his lips. Then he sighed.

"Socrates asks questions about us. He asks about our government. Are we doing the true good? Are we virtuous? Is our government honest?" Eurmikos asked.

Eurmikos was gesturing as he talked. Then he stopped. He took a breath.

"Socrates asks *everyone* questions like that," Eurmikos went on. "Some people get angry. They get worried. Especially the government leaders. They'd rather just live life without thinking. Or trying to be good. But Socrates forces them to see themselves as they are."

No wonder people wanted to kill Socrates, Kenneth thought. No one liked to see the ugly truth about himself. After all, *he* got mad when the coach told him he'd messed up a play—even when he knew the coach was right.

"I get it," Aleesa said. "It's like when Grandma makes me admit that I—aiiieee!" she squealed. Kenneth had just poked her hard. She glared at him.

"So some leaders feel threatened," Eurmikos continued. He gave Aleesa a puzzled look. "Like our leaders Anytus and Meletus. They think Socrates could even overthrow our government. Just by talking and asking questions!"

Eurmikos laughed wryly. But then his smile vanished.

This wasn't like their own time in the U.S., Kenneth thought. Americans could say just about anything they wanted about the government. Except people still didn't like to admit when they were wrong. Or didn't know anything. *That* sure hadn't changed.

"The *boule* will bring charges of crimes against Socrates today," Eurmikos went on. "They will think of something. Maybe that he is turning the youth against the government. They'll say he should be—put to death," Eurmikos said heavily.

"Put to death?" Aleesa asked. Sure, she knew that. And he *would* be put to death too. It gave her shivers.

Eurmikos went on. "Socrates is allowed to answer the charges. Then he will be tried. The *boule,* our 500 man council, will vote guilty or innocent. After that, Socrates can even suggest a different punishment if he's found guilty."

"But Socrates is such a good man!" Kenneth blurted out. "It's not fair he's going to die!"

41

Eurmikos looked at Kenneth strangely. "No one said Socrates *would* die," Eurmikos said. "He may win. The *boule* may vote him innocent. Why do you think he will die?" he asked curiously.

Kenneth felt a huge clamp tighten in his stomach. What a jerk he was! Quick! he commanded himself. Think of something. Quick!

"I . . . I mean, Tisander said he'd make sure Socrates would die, didn't he?" Kenneth stammered. He held his breath for a second.

Would Eurmikos believe his answer? Or were they going to be found out?

5

Socrates' Charges

Eurmikos looked at Kenneth oddly for a moment. Kenneth could feel his heart pounding. Please, he begged silently.

"Hmmm," Eurmikos said. He stroked his beard. "Well, yes," he said. "Tisander did threaten Socrates, didn't he?"

Kenneth felt a wave of relief wash over him. Whew! Eurmikos didn't suspect he and Aleesa were from another place and time.

"Tisander is just a foolish youth," Eurmikos sighed. "He's just a few years older than you two."

"Why does Tisander think that way?" Aleesa blurted out. "His father, Laios, likes Socrates, right?"

"Yes, Laios is one of Socrates' good friends," Eurmikos replied. "And Laios's daughter, Eleni, likes Socrates also." Then Eurmikos's face darkened. "But then there's Tisander." He shook his head. "Tisander used to be a good boy. But he has bad friends. And he thinks he has to rebel to prove he's a man." Eurmikos snorted. "A month ago, Socrates made him feel very bad with his questioning. Tisander didn't want to admit he was wrong. Ever since then, he's hated Socrates."

Shouting broke out in the street. Through the open door, Aleesa heard voices yelling.

"The charges! They've made the charges!"

"Socrates is doomed!"

A man flung himself into the doorway. His *chiton* was rumpled. His eyes were glassy.

"Meletus made the charges!" the man cried out. Everyone in the shop stopped talking. The potters' wheels turned to a stop.

Aleesa felt a knot tie in her stomach. She was afraid to hear what he would say. This was an awful feeling. She squeezed her hands together.

Kenneth stared at the man. His mouth felt dry. He knew what was going to happen to Socrates. *If* he and Aleesa didn't do anything about it.

"What are the crimes he's charged with?" Eurmikos asked hoarsely.

"First, he is charged with not believing in the gods of Athens. They say he brought in new religious ideas. Second, he is charged with corrupting the young people of Athens. He is turning them to evil ways," the man gasped out.

Huh, Kenneth thought. Those were pretty wild charges. What could Socrates do?

"And what is the penalty they are asking?" Eurmikos asked, shaking his head.

"Death!" the man exclaimed. "They say they'll put Socrates to death if he's found guilty."

The man rushed back out into the street. They could hear his voice shouting in the next shop.

"Death!" Aleesa said loudly. She looked at Kenneth. "What can we do now?" she asked.

Eurmikos looked at her curiously. "What can *you* do?" he asked. "That's a strange question."

Kenneth jabbed her with his elbow. Aleesa made a face at Kenneth. Shut up! she wanted to snap at him.

"She means, what happens now?" Kenneth said quickly. He held his breath. Would Eurmikos believe him again?

"Ah, of course," Eurmikos said. "It is as I told you. Now Socrates answers the charges. Then the trial will happen. But not right away."

"When does the *boule* vote him guilty? I . . . I mean, when is the trial?" Kenneth asked.

"Socrates has a little time before the trial," Eurmikos said. "Some weeks, perhaps more. Then the *boule* votes after the trial. I think he should leave Athens forever before the trial. Go into exile. In fact—"

Eurmikos stopped. He bent down a little. He lowered his voice.

"I think that's what our leaders Anytus and Meletus really want Socrates to do," Eurmikos confided. "I don't really think they want to put him to death. They know he is truly a good man. Most people do know that. They just want him out of the way. He causes too much trouble for them in the government with his questions."

"But, no! He really does end up—" Aleesa began to blurt. Kenneth kicked her under the table. "Ow!" she exclaimed. She reached down. She rubbed her shin. What a jerk! she snapped silently.

"Ah, she means, he really does want to stand trial, right?" Kenneth broke in smoothly. "Socrates would want the truth to come out. He's no coward, right?" Kenneth darted a heated glance at Aleesa. He was sure getting tired of cleaning up after her.

"Yes," Eurmikos answered. He glanced at Aleesa. Aleesa's face was bright red. She still rubbed her shin.

Eurmikos lowered his voice again. "But I think Laios and some other friends of Socrates may make other plans for him," he said mysteriously. Then he brightened. "Well, it is time to close shop for the day," he said. He turned to the others. He clapped his hands. "Finished!" he called out.

"You'll be going to Laios's house, right?" Eurmikos asked. "He said you're staying with him. Eleni, his daughter, is coming with a servant to get you."

Whew! Aleesa thought. At least they had a place to live. Until they could figure out how to get back home. She frowned. So what were they going to do about Socrates? she asked herself. She began cleaning up the extra bits of clay. She wiped up her side of the table with a damp cloth.

"Here's Eleni now," Eurmikos said. He pointed to the doorway.

"*Hail!*" said a girl about Aleesa's age, smiling. A servant stood behind her. Eleni wore a *chiton* too. Aleesa noticed it had a pretty design on the hem and sleeves. She looked down at her own *chiton*. It was plain. Oh, well, she thought. No malls in Athens. Looked like she was stuck with this.

"Hurry," Eleni was saying to them. "Socrates is going to answer the charges. I want to hear him," she added.

Aleesa and Kenneth finished cleaning up hurriedly. They said good-bye to Eurmikos. They followed Eleni out of the shop. She smiled at them.

"My father said you two were good people," Eleni said. "I hope you feel the way I do about Socrates." A look of sadness crossed her face. "I feel so bad. I hope he can win this trial. Follow me," she urged.

Eleni walked quickly. She dodged a donkey pulling a cart filled with pottery. Eleni, Kenneth, and Aleesa threaded their way through the crowded, noisy streets.

"The council meets on the next hill," Eleni called over her shoulder.

Together, the three quickly climbed the incline. Aleesa stared around her. On the next hill she could see that famous building! A chill ran through her. Imagine— she was right here! What was the name of it, anyway? It had a long and funny name. Its white columns gleamed in the bright sunlight. It overlooked the city of Athens.

Kenneth blinked in the bright sunlight. He stared in shock at the buildings. Here they were, right in the middle of what they'd been studying about. The Greeks were supposed to build such beautiful buildings. He'd always thought that was kind of dumb. To think a building was pretty.

Kenneth looked at the Parthenon on the next hill. They really *were* kind of nice-looking buildings. No junky-looking neon signs or McDonald's golden arches around here, for sure.

Kenneth tugged at Aleesa's robe. He pointed to the Parthenon. "Bet you don't know the name of that!" he teased. "Ms. F-on-the-test!"

Aleesa slapped his hand away. "Fine!" she snapped. "I suppose *you* do!" she challenged.

"The Parthenon," Kenneth almost crowed. "Ha! Gotcha!"

"All right," Eleni called. "Here we are." Kenneth, Aleesa, and Eleni joined a huge crowd. They could see hundreds of men standing in what looked like part of a stadium. In the center, they saw Socrates. The small, chubby man stood on a small mound.

"Shhhh," Kenneth hissed to Aleesa. "He's already talking." Aleesa made a face at him. She turned her back on Kenneth and listened. A hush had fallen over the crowd.

"And for the first crime. How can you say first that I do not believe in gods?" Socrates was saying. "And yet then you say that I am teaching new gods?" He shook his head with a smile. "Your charges contradict each other. How can I teach new gods if I don't believe in gods at all?" he asked.

Whoa! Aleesa thought. She elbowed Kenneth. She nodded her head in agreement. Socrates was really smart.

"As for the second crime you charge me with," Socrates began.

Socrates turned, speaking to everyone in the crowd. He spread out his arms.

"That I corrupt the young." Socrates sighed. "Young people will always question their elders. Perhaps they do not give enough respect to their elders. But I have not taught them to do this. I have no official students. Remember, I take no money from those I talk with. I am not a teacher. And these are only youthful spirits. Who among you did not question your elders when you were young?"

"Not bad," Kenneth whispered to Aleesa. He raised his eyebrows. "No wonder Socrates is so famous." Aleesa nodded.

"Let's go home," Eleni said, after the council began disbanding. Little knots of men stood talking. Some voices were angry. Some sounded sad.

Everyone sure had a strong opinion about Socrates, Aleesa thought. She swallowed hard. He really was a good person. He sure knew how to use words to win. He didn't want to hurt people. She could see that. He just wanted them to think hard about what they did.

She hurried after Eleni and Kenneth. They pushed their way through the crowd.

And if Kenneth wanted to try to stop him from dying, well, she'd help too, Aleesa told herself. Maybe they could change history after all. Kenneth had a point. They'd already changed history just by being here, right?

Yes. They'd try to save Socrates, Aleesa repeated silently. Somehow. Even if it meant they might not get home for a while. Then her forehead throbbed in time with her pulse.

If they *ever* got home.

6

Socrates Chooses to Stay

Eleni, Kenneth, and Aleesa kept pushing their way through the throngs of people. Eleni's servant followed. They hurried down busy streets. Finally, they stopped in front of a large house fronting a crowded street. There were no windows. A door with a huge bar greeted them. Eleni lifted the knocker.

51

Thud! Thud! The sound echoed hollowly.

"Yes, mistress," a servant said, swinging open the door.

"Come," Eleni said. Kenneth and Aleesa followed. A sunny courtyard lay in the middle of the house. Aleesa recognized roses and violets growing. A fountain splashed in the center.

"The men's quarters are there," Eleni said. She pointed to rooms on the left. "The women's quarters are over here." She gestured to the right. "We won't see Kenneth again until tomorrow."

"What?" Aleesa squeaked. She didn't want to be stuck in ancient Athens all by herself! Even being with Kenneth was better than being alone.

Eleni looked puzzled for a moment. "Your customs in Ionia are different?" she asked. She shrugged her shoulders. "Here in Athens, women are kept separate. We stay home most of the time. My father lets me go out sometimes, though," she added. "I can go to the shop. Or I can go hear the *boule*. That's why I could hear Socrates. Otherwise I weave and stay at home. The men can go out to the market, the *agora*. They can go to the gymnasium. But not us."

Aleesa's jaw dropped. And she thought living with Grandma was bad!

"Yeah," Kenneth proclaimed. "That sounds about right!" He grinned wickedly at Aleesa. "Guys go out. Girls stay home."

"You shut up, Kenneth," Aleesa fumed. "You'll get yours. You just wait." She folded her arms. She pressed her mouth together tightly.

"In your country, the marriages are arranged, true?" Eleni asked.

"What?" Aleesa squawked. "Nuh-uh. No way. We always—unh!" Kenneth poked Aleesa in the side. She whipped around and glared at him.

"That's different," Eleni said. "That's too bad. Arranging marriages is a good idea," she said. She looked at Aleesa. "Maybe my father could arrange a marriage for you while you're here," Eleni offered. "You are the age to be married. So am I." She smiled. "I hope my father will pick a nice, rich, older man for me."

Aleesa stood, frozen. This was a nightmare! Kenneth started laughing.

"Great, Aleesa!" Kenneth gasped in between hoots of laughter. "An old married woman!" He doubled over with laughter.

Aleesa gave him a shove. "Shut up, Kenneth," she snapped. "You're not so funny." She looked at Eleni. "Uh, maybe not," Aleesa said quickly. "I don't think it's a good idea."

"Well, we'll see," Eleni said hopefully. "I will go to the kitchen and have the servants bring something for us to eat." Her robes rustled across the courtyard tiles.

Kenneth's face was red from laughing. Tears ran down his cheeks. He was pointing at Aleesa.

"That's a good one! You won't have to go to the mall to meet guys anymore!" Kenneth hooted.

She'd just like to slap him one, Aleesa told herself. She gritted her teeth.

"Quit making such a big deal about it," Aleesa hissed. "They'll find us out! And then how are we going to save Socrates?" she asked.

Kenneth quit laughing. He wiped his eyes. He walked closer to Aleesa. He looked around. No one was there.

"You decided we should try, then?" Kenneth asked. He crossed his arms.

"Yeah," Aleesa said. "Socrates really is a good man. And he's smart too. He shouldn't have to die for some stupid reason."

Aleesa frowned down at the courtyard paving. She traced a tile pattern with her toe.

"But I don't know what we can do. Should we tell him what's going to happen? That everyone will vote guilty? That he'll die?" Aleesa asked, earnestly.

Kenneth frowned. "No," he said. "Why would he believe us? I mean, he's smart, but there's no way he'd believe who we really are. Besides, we can't tell anyone anything. Who knows what the *boule* might charge *us* with? Then we won't be able to help him at all." Kenneth sighed.

"Greetings, young people," Laios's voice said behind them. He walked into the courtyard. He sat on a carved stone bench. He looked up at Kenneth and Aleesa.

"What did you think of Socrates today?" Laios asked. "I saw you there with Eleni."

"He was great!" Kenneth answered. "I didn't know he was so smart!"

"It's so sad they want him to die!" Aleesa said. She twisted her hands together. "Isn't there anything we can do?" she asked.

Laios glanced behind him. "Tisander is still at the gymnasium throwing the discus," he said. "With his friends."

Laios pressed his mouth together. Then he motioned them to come closer.

"Yes," Laios said in a low voice. "There is something we can do. Some of my friends and I are going to talk to Socrates. We want him to leave Athens. He can do that, you know. He can just leave. He could never come back, though."

"But, won't they send the cops . . . I . . . I mean *someone* after him?" Aleesa stammered. She felt her face flush. "To catch him and bring him back?"

Whoa! Aleesa flinched. She almost messed that one up good. She didn't dare even look at Kenneth after that comment.

"Actually," Laios said. "No. I truly think that Anytus and Meletus just want Socrates to leave Athens too. I don't really think they want to put him to death. They just want him out of the way. Socrates causes too much trouble for them. He makes the government look stupid sometimes." Laios shook his head. "Socrates is just that way."

"So, you're going to talk to Socrates? You'll try to convince him to leave? Before the trial even starts?" Kenneth asked.

Laios nodded. Kenneth exchanged glances with Aleesa. She gave him a thumbs-up signal. Kenneth took a deep breath. "Can . . . can we come too?" he asked. He watched Laios's face.

Laios looked puzzled for a moment. "I suppose so," he said. He looked at Aleesa. "Usually, Athenian girls stay at home," he said.

Aleesa opened her mouth to say something. Kenneth shot her a glance. She snapped her mouth shut. Fine, she thought. She'd be quiet *this* time.

"But you're a *metic*," Laios said to Aleesa. "You're different." He smiled. "And you care for Socrates. You can come also." He stood up. "We have no time to waste," he said. "Let's go to Socrates. He'll be at the painted *stoa*. Near the *agora*."

Laios hurried through the door. Kenneth and Aleesa followed. Laios walked briskly through the narrow streets. The setting sun cast purple shadows on the bright white buildings. Kenneth and Aleesa dodged potholes. They avoided mule-drawn carts.

"There!" Laios said. He pointed. Ahead must be the painted *stoa*, Kenneth thought. On the wall behind the columns were painted beautiful decorations and figures.

Socrates was just leaving a small group of men. They were laughing. Socrates was smiling.

They were really going to talk to Socrates! Kenneth realized. His heart began to pound. What were they going to say? They'd better be careful about what they said. Could they save Socrates? Would this be their only chance? He frowned at Aleesa. He held his finger to his lips.

Aleesa turned the corners of her mouth down. Then she mouthed the word "Okay" silently to Kenneth. She wasn't going to mess up this time. She'd be quiet. Socrates was a great man. She didn't want him to die.

"Greetings, Socrates," Laios said. He lowered his voice. "May we speak freely?"

"If such a thing can be done in Athens these days," Socrates said with a sigh. He smiled gently. "Speak, friend."

Laios looked around him. Men were busy in their own conversations.

"Socrates, you have many friends," Laios began.

"Perhaps not in the *boule,*" Socrates joked. "Certainly not Anytus. Nor Meletus."

"Well, you do have friends," Laios said. "We want you to leave Athens. We want you to go into exile. Anytus and Meletus don't really want to put you to death. Why don't you just leave? Avoid the trial? You can live a longer life."

It made good sense, Kenneth thought. *He'd* go if he had the chance. He looked at Socrates and waited.

Socrates shook his head. "No, friends," he said. "You must try to understand. First of all, it is possible that I could win the trial. But even if I lose, I cannot leave. I believe in the Athenian state. I believe in the government. I believe in democracy."

Socrates' voice was strong. He raised his fist in the air. Aleesa backed up a step. She could tell he really believed what he was saying. She and Kenneth exchanged glances.

"What would it say about me if I left like a coward?" Socrates asked. "That everything I'd said was a lie! It would mean that I didn't believe in democracy! If the Athenian council thinks it must put me to death, I must agree with its rules. I will not go back on my own beliefs. I must be a good citizen. Act honorably and truthfully. Accept laws."

"Whoa!" Kenneth burst out. Both Laios and Socrates looked at him.

Socrates burst out laughing. "Young man! You find it strange that I should be willing to die for my beliefs? I live by them. I should die by them too."

Socrates glanced at the setting sun. "It is getting late. My lovely wife Xanthippe will be angry. I can't be late again. She'll throw another bowl of water on me!" He chuckled. "Getting along with Xanthippe is good training. It makes it easier to get along with all kinds of people," he joked.

Aleesa giggled in spite of herself. How could Socrates still have a sense of humor? His life was in danger. But he seemed to have no fear. That was amazing. She looked over at Kenneth. He was grinning too.

"Farewell," Laios said. He raised a hand. Socrates did the same.

Slowly, Laios, Kenneth, and Aleesa walked back to Laios's house. The servant let them in through the heavy wooden door. Laios disappeared into the men's quarters. Kenneth and Aleesa stood alone in the open hall.

"There you are, you *metics!*" a rude voice called from the courtyard. "I bet you've been talking with Socrates the traitor!"

Kenneth and Aleesa looked at each other. Great, Aleesa thought. That jerk Tisander.

Kenneth doubled up his fists from habit. He'd better watch it. He couldn't touch Tisander.

Tisander stood in the center of the courtyard. His arms were folded. His brows were knitted in anger.

"Have you heard?" Tisander challenged. "Socrates thinks he might win at the trial." He narrowed his eyes. "He's all talk and no action. Talk, talk, talk. But that's where it ends. That man shouldn't be walking the streets of Athens," he said with menace in his voice. "If he wins, he'd better be careful."

Tisander stared at Kenneth and Aleesa.

"And you'd better be careful too," Tisander threatened.

7

Tisander's Threat

"Those weeks before Socrates' trial went too fast," Kenneth said to Aleesa a few weeks later. "It's hard to believe the trial is going on right now. Right now!" he added. His face reflected his worried tone. "In fact, it might even be over already."

Kenneth and Aleesa sat at the low table in the pottery shop. All around them, workers were busy shaping and painting vases. The whine of the potters' wheels filled the air. A fine dust sifted over the tables.

"I wish we could be watching the trial. But, of course, we have to work," Kenneth grumbled. "But we've got to find out what's happening."

"I know," Aleesa said, frowning. She poked at the clay coil she was working on.

Aleesa dug the clay scraper into the clay, making little grooves. She looked at Kenneth, worry creasing her forehead.

"You know what else is making me nervous?" Aleesa asked in a low voice. "Every day when we walk through the *agora,* I've been looking for the cheese lady. So we can get back home. But I haven't seen her." She thumped the clay scraper down in disgust. "This is a mess," she sighed. "Everything's a mess. Do you think Socrates will win?" she asked.

Kenneth rested his chin on his hands for a second. "Well, in history, he didn't," he said slowly. "But then, *we* weren't in Athens in history either." He shook his head. "I don't know what to think."

"I know," Aleesa said. "Socrates is so smart. I can't believe he wouldn't win in the trial!"

"Guilty! Guilty!" voices shouted outside the shop. "Socrates is guilty!"

Aleesa and Kenneth stared at each other. Aleesa felt her heart sink.

"No!" Aleesa said softly. To her surprise, she blinked back tears. "This can't be happening. He's too good a person." She shut her eyes.

"Socrates was found guilty," Laios said loudly, walking into the shop. He looked tired, Kenneth thought.

Everyone fell silent. Kenneth watched all the workers put down their tools and clay. A growing sense of doom crept over him. This was too much like what really happened in history, he told himself.

"What happened?" Aleesa asked. "Tell us, please!"

"The *boule* voted him guilty. He argued well. But they didn't listen," Laios said.

Laios took off his cloak. He sighed and laid it on a table.

"There was much he could have said in defense," Laios went on. "About his courage in battle for Athens. How he has defended people. But he wouldn't do that. He talked only about the charges. He did the honorable thing. But it will be the death of him."

Laios dropped down heavily onto a wooden stool. He put his head in his hands for a moment. Then he looked back up. The shop was silent. No one moved.

"The members of the *boule* still remembered the story of the Oracle at Delphi," Laios sighed. "That was when someone asked the Oracle if Socrates was the smartest man in Athens. The Oracle answered yes! And then Socrates' answer made people mad. He replied it was probably true because he was the only man in Athens who admitted he didn't know anything."

Kenneth grinned. "That's great!" he whispered to Aleesa.

"Yeah," Aleesa answered. "But it didn't help him, did it? It made people mad at him."

Laios was still talking. "And so the judges asked for the death penalty. Then, as you know, Socrates could have suggested another penalty instead. Meletus and Anytus were still hoping he would ask for exile, I think. The *boule* would have voted for that."

"What happened, master?" Eurmikos called from the back of the shop. "Did Socrates suggest banishment instead? Exile from Athens?"

Laios frowned. "You know Socrates. He always speaks the truth." Laios shook his head. "I still cannot believe he did this. But he did."

"What?" Kenneth and Aleesa burst out together. They looked anxiously at Laios, waiting for his answer.

"Socrates said that his penalty should be a medal!" Laios exclaimed. "He said he should get a reward for being such a help to Athens and its citizens, for helping them think. He wanted the same reward the Olympic athletes get for victory! He asked for a lifetime seat at the Prytaneum table!" Laios sighed. "Not a death penalty! But a reward!"

"What a rebel!" Aleesa whispered, her eyes shining. "He just really says the truth!"

"Yeah, but look what happens," Kenneth reminded her. He pressed his mouth into a thin line.

"Well, that did it," Laios continued. "After that, nearly everyone in the *boule* voted for the death penalty. They were angry at his attitude about the reward." Laios shook his head. "Now he is in the prison. Now he must die."

Kenneth and Aleesa looked at each other.

"When?" Kenneth burst out. "When does he die?" He clenched his fists. They were going to have to do something fast. Especially if they were going to try to change history.

"Usually it's right away," Laios said. "Within twenty-four hours. But he cannot be put to death yet. The sacred boat hasn't come back from Delos yet. We can have no executions until it comes back. And it may come back any day. Then he will die."

Still shaking his head sadly, Laios walked to the drying racks. He began looking at the vases. He picked up a vase. He turned it around and around, studying the paintings.

Work began again in the shop. Voices began quiet conversation. Potters' wheels hummed and whined.

"Let's go talk to Laios," Kenneth whispered. "I bet he's already thinking of a way to get Socrates out of this. And we've got to help. Remember, we could be here in Athens just for that reason," he said. "We have to change history."

"I know," Aleesa agreed. "I don't want Socrates to die." She frowned. "That just isn't right. That someone so good has to die."

Aleesa sighed. She fingered her *chiton*. "You know what else?" she added. "I'm getting really tired of this Athens stuff. I want to go home." She stared down at her robe. "I miss my Levis. And my friends. And the mall. Even Grandma," she added, making a face.

"I told you we had to wait," Kenneth reminded her. "Until we found out what happened in the trial. And you want to save him as much as I do." Kenneth got up. Aleesa followed.

"I know. I know," Aleesa pouted. "I do. But let's hurry up and get it done. So we can get back home."

Kenneth and Aleesa walked over to Laios. He was admiring a vase.

"Um, Laios, sir," Kenneth began. He lowered his voice. "Is there anything we can do about Socrates? To keep him from dying, I mean?"

"Some of us were talking after the trial today," Laios said. He looked around. No one in the shop listened. "We are going to arrange for an escape from the prison. If Socrates will agree, that is." Laios rapped his fingers on the vase. "He may not. But we will try."

"We want to help!" Aleesa said. She clenched her hands at her sides. "We'll do anything!"

Laios smiled at her. "You have seen the true goodness of this man, haven't you, my child?" he said.

Just then, Tisander and his friends burst into the shop. Tisander swaggered over to Laios.

"See?" Tisander crowed. "Socrates couldn't save himself!" He looked at his father. "You always said he does the right thing. Well, what about now?" he argued.

Kenneth and Aleesa backed away a few steps. She wasn't going to get in the middle of this, Aleesa thought. Nuh-uh. Tisander's timing was pretty bad.

Tisander's friends shuffled closer behind him. Some of them hid snickers behind their hands. What a bunch of losers, Kenneth thought. He set his jaw. There had better not be any trouble.

Laios frowned at his son. "You give away your age, my son. You are not acting like the adult you wish you were." He looked around at the faces in the small circle of his friends. Then he went on. "You and your young pup friends need to grow up. Until then, you will be treated like the children you still are."

Laios put the vase down. He stared for a long moment at his son. Then Laios turned on his heel. He walked out of the shop.

Aleesa watched Tisander's face flush. He glanced at his friends. They looked furious too, Aleesa thought. Tisander swiveled his head around to stare at her and Kenneth. She drew in a quick breath.

"The *metics!*" Tisander blustered. "Not working again! Lazy!" He narrowed his eyes. "And you support a traitor, I hear. You think Socrates is a great man," he jeered. Then he stepped closer. He lowered his voice. "You'd better watch out," he threatened. "Sometimes bad things happen to *metics*. They're not really citizens of Athens, you know."

Tisander looked around at his friends. They nodded their heads in agreement. Some of them muttered under their breath. Then Tisander looked back at Kenneth and Aleesa. A sneer crossed his face.

"Sometimes *metics* are kidnapped in the middle of the night," Tisander said in an ugly voice. "They're sold into slavery." He straightened up. "Now wouldn't that be a shame!"

8

Pottery Shop Ruins

All night, Aleesa tossed on her cot. Her heart pounded at every little noise she heard. Eleni had told her that house walls in Athens were made of dried mud. Burglars could dig right through them!

Aleesa shivered under her thin cover. Would Tisander

send someone to dig through the walls? Tisander's threat still rang in her ears.

Would someone kidnap her? Sell her into slavery? At least there were no windows someone could climb into. Aleesa squeezed her eyes shut and prayed for sleep to come.

In his room in the men's quarters, Kenneth stared at the ceiling. Tisander's words ran through his mind. Would Tisander pay someone to capture them?

Kenneth's forehead throbbed. No way would he let that happen. He hadn't done all that weight training in football for nothing. Tisander and his friends were wimps. He'd turn all of them into dog meat.

Morning finally came. Aleesa rubbed the sleep from her eyes. Groggily, she got ready. She walked out into the open courtyard. The early morning sky was rinsed pale blue. The sun still hid behind the low roof. She shuffled into the dining room she and Kenneth used with the servants.

Kenneth already lay on one of the eating couches. He was eating fruit and bread.

The first time they'd gone into the dining room, Aleesa had started laughing. "We're gonna eat lying down?" she asked.

"Shhhhh!" Kenneth had warned her. Aleesa had crinkled up her nose at him, of course. He always thought he knew everything.

Now Aleesa was getting used to it. But it still seemed weird.

Aleesa dropped down on a couch. She looked over at Kenneth. He had dark circles under his eyes.

"You look tired," Aleesa said. She lowered her voice. "Were you thinking about the same thing I was last night?" she asked.

"Yeah," Kenneth muttered. "Unless you were thinking about what sales you were missing at the mall." He popped a couple of grapes into his mouth. "I was worried about that jerk, Tisander," he whispered. "But even more than that, I was wondering how we're going to save Socrates' life."

"I hope Laios comes up with a good plan for escape," Aleesa said. "It had better be soon too. We don't know when that boat will show up, right?" She shuddered a little. "It could even be coming into port right now. Then it'll be too late. Socrates will die." A chill went down her back.

Aleesa took a knife. She sliced off some bread. She began to put it into her mouth.

A commotion broke out in the courtyard. Voices yelled. Heavy doors slammed.

"Help! Help! Ho!"

"Trouble! Trouble in the shop!"

Kenneth and Aleesa stared at each other. Kenneth jumped up. Aleesa followed, dropping her bread.

"What's happening?" Aleesa asked, hurrying behind Kenneth. They reached the inner courtyard. They stopped at what they saw.

Servants ran back and forth. Some carried huge baskets. Others carried brooms.

Kenneth grabbed someone. "What happened?" he asked. "What's everyone doing?"

The man looked at him, his eyes wide. "The pottery shop!" he exclaimed. "Someone broke into it! They smashed everything! Laios is nearly ruined!" Then he rushed through the main doorway.

"Oh, no!" Aleesa gasped. She looked at Kenneth. "Are you thinking what I'm thinking?" she asked. "Tisander and his friends?"

"Uh-huh," Kenneth said, his face grim. He set his jaw. "This sounds like something Tisander would pull, doesn't it?" He flexed his fingers. "Those scumball friends of his too. They need to be taught a lesson." He ground his fist into his palm.

Then Kenneth stopped. He frowned. "But hold it. You know, that couldn't be right. Is Tisander that stupid? Is he that bad? Would he wreck his own father's shop? That would just hurt him too, wouldn't it?"

Aleesa leaned against a pillar. She shut her eyes against the morning sun. "I'm thinking," she said. She creased her forehead. "Well, if he was mad enough at his dad, right? For calling him a kid?" She hesitated. "I mean, think of some of the things kids at school have done to their families."

Aleesa looked at Kenneth. He was standing with his arms folded watching her. He just waited.

"Well, maybe not," Aleesa said slowly. "Maybe you're right. Tisander was mad. But I don't think he's stupid. And it'd be stupid to wreck your own shop. What would he do for a living?"

"Well, whoever it was, we'd better get going. We'll have to help clean up," Kenneth said. He started toward the door.

"So responsible!" Aleesa mocked. But she hurried to catch him.

Kenneth and Aleesa heard the uproar at the shop all the way down the narrow street. Voices shouted. Loud thuds sounded. Aleesa heard large objects crash down on the ground. She winced at the ringing sound of crushed vases and dishes being tossed away.

All their work! Aleesa thought. She and Kenneth had finally gotten good at the *hydria* handles. And now it sounded like everything was lost.

When they finally got to the open doorway, Aleesa and Kenneth stopped. They stared inside at the shop.

The color drained from Aleesa's face. No. It wasn't possible. She looked around. Dozens of beautiful vases smashed. Pots and dishes crushed to bits. Tables overturned. Everywhere, workers scurried, trying to clean up.

"I didn't think it would be this bad!" she wailed to Kenneth. She twisted her hands together.

"Me, neither," Kenneth said. He could hardly believe what he saw. This was awful.

"My two *metics*," Laios's voice said behind them.

They turned around. Laios stood, his arms folded across his chest. His face was dark with anger.

"Do you know who did this?" Laios asked. He glared at them.

Kenneth's stomach tied in a knot. He didn't like the way this was starting out. What was Laios thinking?

"N-n-no!" Aleesa stammered. Against her will, her hands shook with fear. Laios didn't think *they* had done it, did he?

"Then why are your eyes wide with fear?" Laios demanded. He looked around him. "I cannot believe you would have done this," he accused.

Kenneth felt as if someone had just punched him in the stomach. "Wait a second!" Kenneth burst out. "You can't say we did this! Why would we? What makes you think so?" He tensed all his muscles, waiting for Laios's answer.

Laios's face relaxed just a bit. He shook his head. "Yes, you are right. Just as I first thought, you must be innocent. You don't act as if you did it." He sighed. "To be honest with you, I couldn't believe it myself," he said. He was still frowning. "But some of Tisander's friends came to tell me just a few minutes ago. They said they'd heard you two plotting something. They said you two were hiding secrets. They keep hearing you say you want to go home. And if there was no work, you could leave. So that's why you'd wreck my shop and go home."

Hiding secrets! Aleesa dug her fingernails into her palm. Going home! Oh, no! Tisander's friends hadn't found out their secret, had they? She felt a sudden stab of panic.

"Plotting!" Kenneth exclaimed in shock. "Yes—but we were trying to figure out a way to save Socrates! Not wreck the pottery shop—that would be stupid!" Stupider than you know, Kenneth added to himself. Then they'd be stuck in an Athenian jail for life. And never get home. "And besides, we were home last night," he added. "The servants know that."

Kenneth glanced at Aleesa. Hiding secrets. Going home. Well, there was more to that than they could ever tell Laios. That was for sure. No one could ever find out where they were really from.

"We'd never do anything like that!" Aleesa cried out. She held her hands out, palms up. "We have to stay here, anyway! We have to help Socrates stay alive," she blurted out.

Laios looked at her carefully. "Yes," he agreed slowly. "I know you have much regard for Socrates. I don't believe that someone who looks up to Socrates would do this."

Laios gestured at the ruined pottery shop. He leaned over. He picked up a piece of a broken vase. He held it out for them to see.

"You know how, on the vases, the artist signs his signature?" Laios pointed at the signature on the vase.

74

"So everyone will know he did the work?" he asked. "Well, this disaster does not have your signature on it," he said. "This did not seem like something you two would do. No matter what Tisander's rude friends claim," he said, frowning.

"Whew!" Kenneth said. Relief washed over him. He felt weak.

"Thanks, Laios," Aleesa blurted out. She was still trembling.

"I think I know enough of you two. I refuse to believe that you would do this." Laios shook his head. Then he looked at them. "But why is it you say you must stay?" he asked. "Is there something you're not telling me?"

Kenneth and Aleesa looked at each other. Great, Kenneth thought. Thoughts flashed through his head at lightning speed. What could he say?

"Uh, no!" Kenneth said quickly. "We—uh—just feel as if we need to stay. To try to save Socrates. He's such a great man." He looked hopefully at Laios's face. Would Laios buy what he was saying?

"Uh-huh," Aleesa chimed in. "He is amazing. We don't want him to die." She held her breath for a second.

Laios broke into a smile. "It is good to see young people like you two and Eleni appreciate Socrates' value," he said. "And I am going to try to take you up on your offer." He lowered his voice. "You want to help Socrates escape. Because you are young, no one will suspect you. You can go to his cell and talk to him. I'll give you the plans we have made." He looked around again. "You can try to talk him into escaping."

Aleesa and Kenneth looked at each other. All right! Kenneth thought. He grinned. This was their chance to change history!

Aleesa smiled, her eyes shining. Maybe *they* could convince Socrates! After all, they knew what really happened. Maybe they could do a better job than the guys who tried to get him to escape in history.

"Good!" Kenneth said. "We'll do it. Just tell us when," he added.

Laios sighed. "We don't have much time," he said. "The boat could come back from Delos any day." He looked around at the shop. "But I have this mess to put to rights also," he said. He shook his head. "I hope I am not ruined. I think enough may have been saved." His face darkened with anger again. "And I must find out who did this. The *boule* will deal harshly with them."

Aleesa and Kenneth exchanged glances again.

Just then, Tisander came bursting through the doorway. "Father! Father!" he exclaimed. He stopped short. He glared at Aleesa and Kenneth.

"I cannot believe you are talking to them!" Tisander shouted angrily. He shook his fist at them. "They are the ones who did this!" he exclaimed. "My friends told me!" He strode over to Kenneth and pushed him against a kiln.

"Whoa, buddy!" Kenneth yelled. He doubled up his

fists. He was gonna pop this guy one for sure. Aleesa grabbed his arm.

"Don't!" Aleesa hissed. "You can't! Not now! Not yet!" Her fingers tightened on his arm. If Kenneth got in trouble, she was doomed too. She flinched.

Kenneth dropped his fists. He stared at Tisander. "You touch me again and you'll pay for it," he threatened.

"Young men!" Laios barked. "That is enough. Emotions are high. We have too much to do. Control yourselves," he ordered.

Tisander looked at his father. He shook his fist. "You don't understand. My friends heard them talking. That's what they told me. And now they've reported Kenneth and Aleesa to the *boule*. They'll be charged and arrested!"

9

Time to Run?

"What?" Kenneth croaked out. "They're coming to arrest us?" He grabbed Aleesa's arm. "What can we do?" His mind was spinning. They were definitely in trouble now.

"I don't want to go to jail!" Aleesa cried out. "I didn't do anything! It's not fair," she wailed. Her eyes widened with fear. Jail! She'd spend the rest of her life in an Athenian jail!

Anger filled Laios's voice. "Your friends," he almost spat out, "are the cause of too much trouble!" He glared at Tisander. "They've put the lives of these two good young people at stake. When are you going to come to your senses about those hoodlums?"

Tisander's jaw hardened. "They're not hoodlums." He lifted his chin. "They're just trying to help Athens. Just like getting rid of Socrates," he added spitefully.

"Getting rid of Socrates will be the worst thing Athens has done yet," Laios warned.

Laios looked at Tisander. Tisander looked down at the ground. He pressed his mouth into a thin line.

His voice like ice, Laios went on. "Because you couldn't handle Socrates' truth, you are resentful. You hate the truth. He made you realize the truth about yourself. You must accept what Socrates said. Then you'll be a man." He shook his head. "You'd better leave before I say something I'll regret."

Tisander, his fists clenched, turned on his heel and strode to the door. His cloak swished behind him.

Laios suddenly looked old and tired, Aleesa thought. Poor guy. It must be tough having a son you disagreed with like that.

Laios sighed. He straightened his shoulders. "We have to do something about you two," he said. "I'll have to hide you. If you're arrested, they won't let you go free until the trial. You're *metics*. You have no Athenian rights. You'd have to go to jail." He narrowed his eyes. "Those ruffian friends of Tisander. They're up to no good."

"Where can we hide?" Kenneth asked. "We can't hide at your house, can we? The authorities will come looking for us there."

"I'll hide you with Bion," Tisander said. "My friend you met in the *agora*. The heavy-set man. He's in on the escape plot too."

"But what happens then?" Aleesa asked. She fought a rising tide of panic. "We can't hide at Bion's forever. We have to get home!" she pleaded.

Kenneth shot her a quick glance. He frowned and shook his head quickly.

"And we have to save Socrates," Kenneth added. His forehead creased with worry. "How can we give Socrates the escape plans now? Won't we get caught if we go to the jail to see Socrates?" he said.

Laios sat down on a bench. "Perhaps you are right. But I cannot be the one to give him any plans. The jailers will be watching me too closely. Nor can any of Socrates' other friends. They will be watched also. That's why we needed you two for help."

"You needed us? Really?" Aleesa asked. Her eyes lit up with excitement. She grinned at Kenneth. They really needed her and Kenneth! They could save Socrates!

"Yes," Laios continued. "We knew the jailers wouldn't know who you were. You're *metics*. And you're young, so you wouldn't be suspected of smuggling plans." He shook his head. "I will have to think about how we can still do this," he sighed.

"Well, don't you think we'd better get out of here?" Kenneth asked. He glanced at the doorway. "Those guys could come in here any second."

"You're right," Laios said. He got to his feet. "Follow me. I'll take you to Bion's. No need to worry about being recognized. No one knows what you look like. You haven't been here that long."

Kenneth glanced at Aleesa. He jerked his head toward the doorway. "Let's go," he said. Together, they followed Laios out into the bright sunlight. The noises of the street swirled around them. They pushed their way through the groups of people walking in the streets.

Aleesa's hurried footsteps echoed her beating heart. Now what was going to happen? Here she was, stuck in ancient Athens, far from her own time. They might get thrown in jail. Maybe they couldn't save Socrates after all. And worst of all, she might never get home!

Aleesa squeezed back tears. She never thought she'd miss Grandma so much. She gulped a breath of air. She swallowed hard.

Laios, Aleesa, and Kenneth walked quickly through the *agora*. Aleesa glanced around her. Colorful fruit, cheeses, and clothing overflowed in the marketplace stalls. People bargained loudly with the sellers. Exotic and strange smells met her nose.

Aleesa tugged at Kenneth's robe. Laios was ahead of them. Kenneth fell back in step with her.

"What do you want?" Kenneth asked crossly. "We gotta keep up. We don't know where we're going."

"Hey!" Aleesa said in a low voice. "Do you think that woman is here? The one who let us taste the cheese? Should we just try to find her? Should we just try to get home now?" she asked, worry twisting her face. "Before we get caught and thrown in jail?"

Kenneth looked disgusted. "What are you thinking?" he asked. He shook his head. "We'll try to help Laios first. We have to help Socrates. Then we'll worry about getting home," he said. "First things first." He pulled at her arm. "Now, let's hurry up!"

Finally, Laios led them to a house off a main street. It had no windows on the street. They stopped in front of a huge metal door. Laios raised the heavy knocker.

Clang! Clang! Clang!

Aleesa jumped. She was already too nervous, she told herself.

A servant let them in. A sunny courtyard, filled with flowers, greeted them. Bion sat on a stone bench. He got up.

"Ah, Laios, you've brought our young friends," Bion said. "Ready to talk about the escape plans?" he asked.

"We're in hiding!" Aleesa blurted out. "We're gonna be arrested!" She wrung her hands nervously.

Kenneth jabbed her with an elbow. "Shhhhh," he

warned. She made a face at him.

"My son's stupid friends have turned their names in to the authorities," Laios said. "These two are being accused of wrecking my pottery shop!" He shook his head in disgust. He sat down on the stone bench. "They cannot hide with me and my family," he said. "I am hoping you will hide them."

"Well, of course," Bion said. "Welcome. I wish the reason for your coming were better. But you are welcome here." He held his arms out at his sides. "As long as you need to stay."

"As long as we need to stay?" Aleesa almost squeaked. She wheeled to look at Kenneth.

"How long are we staying?" Aleesa asked. Her heart fluttered a little. How long was all this going to take? Would they ever get home?

"Uh—until things quiet down," Kenneth said. He looked at Laios and Bion. "We—we still want to help with Socrates too. Is it too late?" he asked.

A puzzled frown creased Laios's forehead. "I don't think so. You can hide here. The authorities will look for you for a few days. But they won't find you. Then they'll stop looking. You are *metics,* after all. They'll just decide you went back to Ionia. Why wouldn't you? So then they'll forget about you."

Aleesa hoped so! She swallowed hard.

"Then when things settle down, we'll plan how you can help Socrates," Laios finished.

"I know!" Kenneth exclaimed. "Once you think it's safe, we can still give Socrates the escape plans, can't we? We'll just go at night. We'll wear hoods over our heads. You've said no one knows what we look like. The jailers won't know either, will they?"

Yeah. No TV programs about being the most wanted in ancient Athens, Aleesa snorted silently. Or TV news broadcasting their faces all over the country. Whew! she thought in relief.

"You're willing to do that, still?" Laios asked. He looked at both Kenneth and Aleesa.

"Of course," Kenneth said. Did he sound more confident than he felt? He looked at Aleesa from the corner of his eye. "We've come this far," he said. "We might as well finish, right? You've said we are the only ones who could make it happen. Everyone else would be watched too closely. Right?"

"You show much courage," Bion said. He clapped Kenneth on the shoulder. He smiled at Aleesa. "Both of you."

Aleesa managed a weak smile. Yeah, she thought. Good thing Laios and Bion couldn't see her knees shaking under her *chiton*.

"I told you these two respected Socrates," Laios said with a smile. "They know he speaks the truth. They know he hates a lie."

"Good. Good," Bion said. "Well, I will hide them here. My servants are trustworthy. You let me know when the authorities stop looking for them. Then we'll get them in to see Socrates in his cell."

"If he hasn't been killed yet!" Aleesa burst out. "How many days until they stop looking for us?" she asked. She twisted the sleeve of her robe in her hands.

"Perhaps only a few days. You are only *metics,*" Laios said. "They won't waste their time on non-citizens."

"But—you're sure? We—we won't be carried off to jail?" Aleesa stammered.

Laios smiled. "No, young one. And I'll send Eleni over to visit you," he said. "She'll miss you." Then he frowned. "As for Tisander. I'll have a talk with him about his friends. It's time he sees them for who they really are." His frown deepened. "And I'm beginning to have my suspicions about who really did wreck the pottery shop."

Aleesa and Kenneth exchanged glances. Uh-huh, Kenneth thought. Laios probably thought it was Tisander's friends too. Was he wondering why they'd wreck the shop?

Finally! Aleesa thought. She was beginning to think Laios didn't have a clue about Tisander's friends. They probably wrecked the shop to get back at Laios. For saying that stuff about Tisander and about them too. Or else they wanted to get Kenneth and her in trouble. She kicked a loose pebble with the toe of her sandal. It skittered toward a flower bed. What a bunch of jerks.

"Come," Bion said. "I'll have one of the servants show you your rooms."

Taking a deep breath, Aleesa followed Bion. Kenneth walked behind her.

How many days would they be shut up here? Kenneth wondered, looking around. It was a pretty nice place, sure. He frowned. But he hated being cooped up.

And Kenneth didn't like thinking the Athenian cops—or whatever they called them—could knock on the door any second. And what if he and Aleesa would be too late to save Socrates?

What if Socrates were already dead by the time they could get there?

Two tense weeks passed filled with worry. The hours dragged slowly. Aleesa and Kenneth watched each day dawn hoping it would bring good news.

Laios came to visit Kenneth and Aleesa with his reports each afternoon. Socrates was still alive. The boat had not returned from Delos yet. But rumors were spreading. It was supposed to be arriving soon.

Eleni came too. She brought stories to tell. And gossip about Tisander and his friends. They were still getting into trouble. But no one had found the two *metics* who had wrecked the shop. The talk in Athens was that Laios's two *metics* had run for home.

At the end of the fifteenth day, Aleesa sighed and

looked up longingly at the deepening blue of the sky.

"Do you think we'll ever get out?" Aleesa complained. "Are we going to spend the rest of our lives here in Athens?"

Aleesa watched the stars come out, one by one, winking. She leaned back against a pillar.

"Maybe we should just sneak out and find that cheese lady in the *agora,*" Aleesa said, turning to look at Kenneth. He was lying on the stone bench tracing patterns in the stone. "Don't you think that's how we can get back home? We should have done that before. We should have just left when we could," she fretted.

"Yeah, maybe," Kenneth said. "Except," he said, sitting up, "then we'd never be able to live with ourselves." He looked at Aleesa. "Think about it. What if we get back to Berkeley and study some more Socrates stuff. And we'll always wonder. Could we have changed history? And we never even tried."

"*If* we get back to Berkeley," Aleesa said sarcastically. She sighed. "Yeah, you're right. Even though I hate to admit it." She made a face. "I know we're doing the right thing."

The heavy knocker on the front door made them jump. "Who is that?" Aleesa asked, her eyes wide. "Laios has already come today!"

"Greetings, friend," Laios's voice called out. They heard Bion welcoming him. Was there a different note in Bion's voice? Kenneth wondered. What was going on?

Then Laios appeared in the courtyard. He carried cloaks in one hand. He was holding a vase in the other. "Here!" he said, holding the vase out to them. "It is time. You go tonight to Socrates."

"It's safe?" Kenneth asked. He stared at the vase. What was that for? he wondered. "What about the *boule?* Do they still want to arrest us?"

"No," Laios said. "I spent all afternoon in council. The authorities said you have fled to Ionia. Back home. So they called off the search. And after you meet with Socrates, you are free to go home, of course."

"Yes!" Kenneth and Aleesa said at the same time. They high-fived each other.

"Strange customs, these Ionians," Bion said to Laios. He shrugged his shoulders.

"This vase has the instructions for the escape painted on it," Laios said. He grinned. "Very clever, isn't it?"

Laios handed the vase to Kenneth. He turned it over in his hands.

"Look, Aleesa," Kenneth said. He pointed to the paintings.

"I get it," Aleesa said. She smiled. "It's like a code. It shows where he's supposed to go. And even what time. See the rooster? See the moon in the sky?" She looked at Laios. "Pretty good," she said admiringly. "I guess Socrates knows where these places are? The chariots? The bridge?"

"Yes," Laios said. "They are well known. Here are

your cloaks," he said, holding them out. "You can almost cover your faces. But the jailers won't recognize you anyway, remember? And they will leave you alone with Socrates. But let's hurry. We have no time to waste. The boat is on its way. Socrates will be put to death soon."

Quickly, Kenneth and Aleesa wrapped their cloaks around them. Kenneth carried the vase. They said their good-byes to Bion.

The streets of Athens were dark. Small groups of people walked in the cool night air. Every now and then, laughter would break out.

The gray stone jail loomed up in front of them. "Here," Laios said. He pressed some coins into Aleesa's hand. "This is for your trip home." He smiled at them.

How nice! Aleesa thought. She stared at the coins gleaming in her palm. Wonder if the Berkeley buses would accept those? She swallowed hard. They didn't even know if they'd be able to get home to Berkeley. Ever.

"I hope you can convince Socrates to escape," Laios was saying. "He listens to youth. He may agree." Laios sighed. "I hope so. I do not want to see him die. And—" He stopped. He looked at both Kenneth and Aleesa. "I am sorry for what happened here. I hope you will speak well of Athens to your fellow countrymen," he added. He raised a hand. "Farewell, my two *metics*," he said. "You are doing a great service to humanity."

Kenneth and Aleesa watched Laios disappear down the street.

"Well?" Kenneth said. A worried frown creased his forehead. "I guess we've gotta do it now, huh?"

Aleesa's stomach churned. "You don't think they'll recognize us?" she asked.

"What are you two doing here?" a voice asked behind them. "Why did my father bring you here?"

10
Death of Lies

Aleesa whipped around. Tisander! He stood there, his cloak thrown over his shoulder. His face was in shadow.

Panic gripped Aleesa. She looked around for an escape. It was too late.

"Tisander!" Kenneth exclaimed. He clenched his

fists. "What are you doing here? So you can tell your friends? And then we get thrown in jail?"

"No!" Tisander said quickly. "No, not at all." He looked down at the ground. He cleared his throat.

"I followed my father to see where he was going," Tisander said. "He's been so secretive lately." Tisander rubbed his neck nervously. "I was afraid he was having meetings about me with some of his friends. I was afraid he's thinking about having me sent away. And actually—" He stopped. He looked down at the ground for a moment. "There's something else. I suppose I should tell you something," he added reluctantly.

Tisander looked back up at Kenneth and Aleesa. He frowned.

"Today, I heard my friends talking. One of them slipped." Tisander's lip curled in disgust. "*They* are the ones who wrecked the pottery shop. They thought they were helping me. Hah," he spat out. "They are no friends of *mine!*"

Aleesa and Kenneth looked at each other triumphantly. "We thought so!" Kenneth exclaimed.

"Yeah, no kidding," Aleesa snapped. "What a bunch of idiots. They almost got us thrown in prison for it. So what are you gonna do about it?"

"Yes, Aleesa's right. What are you going to do now? Do you think they did the right thing?" Kenneth asked.

"No. Of course not," Tisander blustered.

"And what should happen to people who do that?"

Kenneth persisted. "What would Socrates say about that? Or do you still think Socrates is a traitor?"

"No. No, I don't," Tisander said. "Not anymore. Since I found out what my friends did, I've been thinking. Especially about Socrates. He asked me hard questions. And in my heart, I knew he was right about me. And about my friends. He is a hard man." He took a breath. "But he expects no less of himself. Look at him now," Tisander said.

Tisander pointed to the jail. Torch light flickered through two small, high windows. Aleesa shivered in spite of herself. It looked scary. And they were supposed to go inside!

"When he could have fled Athens, he didn't. He stayed. He's not a coward. He stands for his beliefs. He lives what he says. My friends did not. I have not. And I fear I've made a big mistake," Tisander admitted. "My father was right about Socrates. Eleni was right. And you two were right."

Tisander stared down at his sandals and sighed. Then he looked back up at Kenneth and Aleesa.

"Yes, I know what you're trying to tell me. And you're right. I should go to the authorities about my friends, shouldn't I?" Tisander shook his head.

"Yeah. You can get them off our backs," Aleesa grumbled. "Just in time for us to go home. We really want to get home."

Kenneth cleared his throat loudly. Aleesa looked at him. Fine! she wanted to snap at him. She wasn't going to give anything away now, was she? They did want to get back home.

Then Tisander looked at them. He looked puzzled. "What *are* you still doing here? I thought you'd gone back home. To get away from the council, the *boule.*"

Aleesa opened her mouth to say something. But Kenneth broke in. She made a face.

"Uh—we're going to visit Socrates," Kenneth said smoothly. "We're giving him this vase. As a farewell gift."

"Oh," Tisander said. He shrugged his shoulders. "Well, good luck to you. I guess I am sad now that Socrates is going to die." He set his jaw a little. "I wish I'd figured the truth out sooner." He raised a hand in good-bye and walked away. His cloak disappeared into the dusk.

"Okay. Let's do this," Kenneth said. He took a deep breath. Could they do it? Would they get caught? He knocked on the heavy door to the jail.

"Yes?" a rude voice called out.

"We're—we're here to see Socrates the prisoner," Kenneth stuttered. "We—we have a gift for him." His mouth felt dry. Calm down, he commanded himself. He fixed his cloak so it shadowed his face.

A grim-looking guard let them in. "Hunh!" he snorted, looking down at the vase. "More young people. Don't be long."

Carrying two lit torches, the guard ushered Kenneth and Aleesa down the long hall. Their footsteps echoed against the stone walls. Kenneth felt sure the guard could hear his heart pounding loudly.

Aleesa followed closely behind Kenneth. She tried to steady her breathing. Her scalp prickled with fear. Was this going to work? Or would they be caught? Her hands felt clammy and her heart raced under her cloak.

The guard opened the door to Socrates' cell. Socrates was sitting on a low chair. He looked up.

"There," the guard growled. "Not long now, you two." He left a torch in the wall bracket.

Thoughts flashed through Kenneth's brain. He took a deep breath. He was going to talk to Socrates. One of the smartest guys in history. What if he said something dumb? What if he and Aleesa couldn't convince Socrates to leave?

A smile lit up Socrates' face. "Ah, my young friends from the pottery shop," he said. "You did not flee after all."

"No, Socrates," Kenneth said. He glanced down the hall. The guard had disappeared. He thrust the vase at Socrates. "Here," he said in a low voice. "Your friends have planned an escape for you. Everything is paid for. The vase has the directions."

"All you have to do is say yes," Aleesa said breathlessly. "Please, Socrates. You could do so much more good. Even in exile. You could help people understand themselves. Even Tisander agrees now."

Socrates smiled gently. "Ah, my children," he said. "You want me to escape. You do not understand. My friends mean well. But they do not understand either."

Socrates leaned back in the chair. He closed his eyes for a moment. Then he opened them. He looked at Kenneth and Aleesa.

"You see, the charges were brought against me by evil men," Socrates explained. "But it was the Athenian government that found me guilty. The *boule* voted me guilty. If I escaped, I would be a traitor. A traitor to the idea of citizenship. My life would be a lie."

Socrates peered up at Kenneth and Aleesa. Then he closed his eyes again. He waited for a second in silence. What was he trying to say? Aleesa wondered. Was he going to refuse?

Socrates began again. "What if everyone agreed to follow laws only if they weren't hurt by them? If we do not agree with our state, can we do anything we want?" Socrates shook his head. "That would be the end of civilization. I must keep my word as an Athenian citizen. I must stay."

"But Socrates," Aleesa begged. "You have so much you could still teach! And I don't want you to die!" She clasped her hands together tightly. He had to say he'd escape. He had to! she told herself.

"Peace, my child," Socrates said. He held up a hand. "Remember that life is a rehearsal for death. In death we are liberated from our bodies. And good men are reunited in a better world. Truth and goodness can be seen face to face. And that is what I want. I have lived a full life. I am seventy now."

"But, Socrates," Kenneth began. He walked closer. "You still have time," he urged. "You can—"

Socrates held up a hand again. He smiled. "No, no. You are honest. You are sincere. I can see that. And I don't doubt my friends' feelings for me. But I cannot end my life a lie. I must show everyone that I live the truth I speak. Know thyself. Remember." He sighed and closed his eyes. "You must go now," he said. "It is getting late."

Kenneth and Aleesa stood up. Aleesa's heart hammered. They were actually saying good-bye to Socrates. She couldn't believe it.

Kenneth stood, rooted to the spot. He couldn't say good-bye. He just couldn't.

"It's terrible you have to die when you aren't guilty," Kenneth choked out.

Socrates smiled. "Would you rather I die and really *be* guilty, then?" He chuckled. "You must go," Socrates said. "Thank you for coming," he added. Then he smiled again. "You must be hungry," he said. "Young people always are. And the *agora* is empty now."

He reached for a plate. Cheeses and bread were piled high.

"My friends tell me to eat well," Socrates said. "They bring me food. They are afraid I will starve."

Socrates laughed. He patted his round belly.

"You'd think they have no eyes," Socrates chuckled. "Here. Have some cheese and bread. The best meal is a plain meal. Take the vase back with you. And good luck on your journey home," he added. "Be true to yourselves. And farewell."

Aleesa took some cheese and bread. She wrapped it in her cloak.

"Good-bye, Socrates," she said slowly. She blinked back sudden tears. Turning quickly, Aleesa took the torch from the wall. She looked down at the ground, waiting for Kenneth.

"Good-bye, Socrates," Kenneth said, gruffly. He cleared his throat. He followed Aleesa.

But halfway down the hall, Kenneth looked back. In the cell, a flickering torch light shone on Socrates' face.

"He looks peaceful, anyway," Kenneth said. He sighed and shook his head. "He really lived what he said. Whew!" he added. "No wonder it was a big deal about Socrates."

"Yeah," Aleesa managed to choke out. "He's really brave. He didn't care what others thought. He was true to himself." She snuffled and wiped her nose on her sleeve.

They left the torch with the guard, being sure to keep their heads down as they talked to him. No use in risking anything now, Kenneth thought.

The cool night air felt good after the clammy air of the prison. Aleesa stopped and stared up at the stars in the black sky. She was free! she thought. Then a horrible thought burst into her brain. She looked at Kenneth in horror.

"Oh, no!" Aleesa exclaimed. "How can we get home? What do we do now? The market is empty. We can't find that lady who sells the cheeses!" Aleesa exclaimed. "Not until tomorrow, anyway." Aleesa gulped a little. "*If* we can find her, that is. And *if* that's how we can get home." She looked worriedly at Kenneth. "And besides, where are we going to sleep tonight?"

Aleesa looked down the dark, forbidding street. A chill wrapped around her.

Kenneth pressed his mouth together for a moment. He stared at the darkened street. "Okay. We'll just go back to Bion's," he said. "Then tomorrow we'll get up early. We'll head for the *agora.* And see if we can find that lady. I'm sure that'll work," he said, trying to sound more confident than he felt.

Would Aleesa believe him? Kenneth sure didn't need her panicking right now. His stomach tied in a knot. What if they couldn't get home? He couldn't even think about it.

"Okay," Aleesa sighed. "Here." She handed him some bread and cheese. "Let's at least have a snack. I'm hungry."

Kenneth took it from her hand. He put a chunk of cheese into his mouth. It tasted—well—familiar. The street began to blur in front of his eyes.

"Hey! Whoa! Aleesa!" Kenneth gasped. He grabbed onto a nearby pillar. A wave of darkness rolled over him. He shut his eyes.

"I know!" Aleesa choked out. Her ears were ringing. The street reeled around her.

"Oh, my gosh! Is it the same cheese?" Aleesa gasped. She fell against a wall and held on to a post. Then everything went black.

A sudden crash of noise made Aleesa blink. She opened her eyes.

Light was everywhere. The street in Athens was gone. Display bins of cheeses, meats, and pickles surrounded them.

It was the store! They were back in the store in Berkeley! Aleesa realized in a daze.

"Hey!" Kenneth said hoarsely. He stared at Aleesa. Then he looked around, stunned. They were back at the grocery store!

"Hey," Kenneth repeated. He lowered his voice. "Did something funny just happen to you?" he asked. He looked carefully at Aleesa. "Really funny. Weird-funny, I mean?" he asked. Was he going crazy? Had this been a dream? he wondered.

Aleesa was rubbing her forehead. She squeezed her eyes shut for a second. "Uh-huh. Something really strange. But I really don't—" she began to say. Then she stopped. She stared at Kenneth.

Her forehead throbbed in time with her pulse. "Socrates," she said hoarsely. "The pottery shop. Look what you're still carrying. It really happened!"

She pointed to what Kenneth still cradled under his arm. Kenneth looked down. His face drained of color. It was the vase.

"Are you kids all right?" the lady behind the cheese tray asked. "You look kind of strange." She looked carefully at Kenneth and Aleesa. "Do you want me to call the manager?" she asked.

Kenneth and Aleesa looked at each other.

"Ah, no . . . no thanks," Kenneth said quickly. "We don't, do we?" He poked Aleesa.

"Ouch!" Aleesa squealed. She stuck out her tongue at Kenneth. "No," she said, turning to the lady. "We're fine. Honest."

Aleesa tried out a fake smile. But her heart still pounded.

"We're really fine." They really would be too, Aleesa thought. Now they'd know a lot about Socrates for the skit. They could bring up their grades.

Aleesa looked at the lady in the costume. Then she thought of something. She smirked to herself.

"Oh," Aleesa added. "One thing." She grinned wickedly at Kenneth. "Can you tell us where to get Greek costumes like that? My friend here wants to wear one in a skit we're doing on Socrates. We're gonna do a great skit and bring up our grades!"

Kenneth grabbed Aleesa by the arm. He pulled her down the aisle away from the cheese lady.

"Funny. Very funny," Kenneth snapped. "No skit. I ain't wearing no dress. I told you that. What makes you think I ever would?" he asked, frowning.

Aleesa smiled. Her eyes danced with fun. "Okay, Mr.

Football Stud. You can't pretend all of that never happened," she said. She knocked on the vase under Kenneth's arm. It rang hollowly.

"Okay. You win," Kenneth said. "I did. But you can never tell anyone. They'll think we're crazy! We'll do the skit. We'll raise our grades." He stopped. "But I ain't wearing—" he began.

"I know," Aleesa broke in.

"No dress!" they said together.

11
Socrates

Before Socrates, people just listened to tradition and superstition and old, outworn beliefs. But because of Socrates' ideas, men began to ask questions instead of just accepting ideas. Socrates believed that people should search for truth and goodness and justice. His ideas changed the world.

Socrates thought that if people knew the truth, they would be truthful. If they really knew and understood what goodness was, they would be good. He felt people should look for the true meaning of justice. And people had only to use their reasoning to find what these ideas were.

In order to help people understand, Socrates asked them questions. He never told anyone answers. He forced people to think for themselves. "Know thyself," was his motto. "The eye of the mind is not blind," he said. "It is merely looking the wrong way."

Socrates is supposed to have been born around 470 B.C. in Greece, in the city-state of Athens. Socrates' parents were good people. His father was a sculptor, or worker in stone carving. Socrates had a good education.

Athenians believed the body was as important as the mind. So Socrates went to the gymnasium and to school.

During his life, Socrates watched Athens grow into a powerful and beautiful city in its "Golden Age." Athens was the first known democracy. The people ruled themselves.

Socrates watched famous works of art begun and completed. The Parthenon was built. Famous plays were written. Pericles was the great leader of Athens.

But then, Athens changed.

Socrates watched Athens fall from the greatness of this "Golden Age" to disaster. War against its enemy, Sparta, sounded the death bell for Athens.

Socrates fought in two wars for Athens. He believed people should be good citizens. He believed they had a duty to their government. He had a good reputation as a fighter. One commander said, "If all my men had been like Socrates, we would have won."

For the first half of his life, Socrates was successful. He was known as a good thinker. Many people knew he was smart. He had a sense of humor. He had many important friends.

A family was also important to Socrates. His wife's name was Xanthippe. They had at least two children.

One day a friend asked the Oracle at Delphi, a priestess of Apollo, if Socrates was the smartest man in Athens. The Oracle replied yes. She felt Socrates was indeed the smartest man in Athens.

When Socrates heard that, he decided he had to prove the Oracle wrong. He knew he wasn't smart. So he went around, trying to find someone wiser than he. All he found were people who *thought* they knew everything. But they really didn't know very much at all.

Then Socrates realized that maybe he *was* the smartest man after all. Out of all the people he talked to, only *he* realized that he didn't know everything!

Socrates became a man with a mission. Maybe what the Oracle was really saying was that people are all ignorant of the one thing they need to know. People need to know how to live a good life.

Socrates decided he should try to show people how important it was to live good lives. He might not know the answer to the question "How should people live a good life?" But at least he knew it was the most important question to ask.

Socrates gave up everything. He lived poorly. He wore one robe all the time. He spent his days talking with people. He questioned them constantly. Of course, some people became angry.

Government leaders became worried. They could see Socrates was asking too many questions. They thought Socrates was criticizing the government. They wished Socrates would leave Athens.

Then an old friend of Socrates, Alcibiades, turned traitor. He told Athenian secrets to Sparta. People were angry with Alcibiades. Sparta fought Athens. Some blamed Socrates.

Athens lost the war against Sparta. Even more

trouble came to Socrates. People felt even more worried and insecure.

A bloodthirsty group called "The Thirty" took over Athens. They killed many people. Unfortunately for Socrates, one of "The Thirty" was an old friend of his. Socrates had nothing to do with this. But some people were out to get Socrates. The government leaders wanted him gone. They thought he was a troublemaker.

Finally, three men brought charges against Socrates. They charged him with not believing in the Athenian gods and with teaching new gods. They charged him with corrupting the young since he encouraged young people to ask questions of their elders.

Socrates could have escaped. But he stayed to face his trial. He argued bravely against the charges. But the council of 500 citizens, the *boule,* voted him guilty. They asked for the death penalty.

By Athenian law, Socrates could have suggested a different sentence. But instead, he told the *boule* that he should be rewarded for helping Athenians think. They were so angry they voted for the death penalty.

Friends of Socrates tried to talk him into escaping. But Socrates refused. He said he would be a traitor if he fled. He believed everything he stood for would become a lie. He was an Athenian citizen and he should behave as a citizen. He should stand up for his beliefs.

Finally, Socrates drank the poisoned hemlock. He died in peace, with his friends weeping at his deathbed.

Socrates never wrote a word. But many of his questions and ideas were written down by one of his students named Plato. They are called the "Dialogues of Plato." In them, Plato talks about Socrates' ideas and how he made people face hard truths. People can read them still today.

Socrates' ideas changed the world and the way people think about themselves.

SOME OF SOCRATES' FAMOUS SAYINGS

"It doesn't matter if you don't have enough food for your guests. If they are reasonable people, they will understand. If they are not reasonable people, you shouldn't care what they think."

"Should someone get married? It doesn't matter what you answer. Whatever choice the person makes, he will live to regret it."

"Some people live only to eat. I eat only to live."

"Better late than never with learning."

"The one evil is ignorance. The one good is knowledge."

"Why do people act badly? Because of bad education and bad friends."

"The good must be something which always benefits and never harms."

"The eye of the mind is not blind. It is merely looking the wrong way."